I0619193

CUCKED AND REPLACED

HOW A RICH BULL CLAIMED MY HUSBAND

JACK HORNWOOD

Cucked and Replaced
How a Rich Bull Claimed My Husband

Jack Hornwood

2nd Edition
Copyright © 2020 Jack Hornwood
ISBN: 978-1-99-117752-0
Written in Aotearoa

www.jackhornwood.com

A MESSAGE FROM THE AUTHOR

Cuckolding is a complicated kink, and sometimes the things that turn you on the most are also the things that hurt the most. Everyone has different boundaries between what's hot because it hurts, and what just hurts too much.

For me, writing erotica has been a way of exploring the things that turn me on but that I might not be able to make happen — and might not *want* to happen — in real life. It's a space to enjoy the fantasy without anyone having to experience the consequences of trying these things in real life.

So this book embraces the stuff that hurts, the stuff that I'm guessing would probably hurt too much if it happened to you in real life. I want to emphasise that this story is fantasy, not role-modelling for how a cuckold relationship should work in the real world.

In real life cuckolding requires huge amounts of trust and ongoing communication. It's about ensuring you are both getting what you need out of it, and checking in to make sure you're both still enjoying it. And it involves setting bound-aries together and sticking to them unless you make a joint decision, together, to shift them.

Look after the people you care about, and make sure they know you respect them no matter where your kinks take you.

CHAPTER 1

Tonight was the second time in a week that I'd found myself driving my husband over to another guy's house for sex. The first time, a couple of nights ago, had been kind of a bust. The guy had shot his load after only a couple of minutes of being fucked, which meant Julian had left unsatisfied. That had worked out okay for me though, because when we'd got home he'd had so much pent up need that he'd bent me over the kitchen table and fucked me right there like a piece of meat. But it was still always disappointing for both of us when one of his hookups didn't work out as planned.

Julian always had a lot of sex. He'd always been that way: highly sexually charged, and always ready to go, with a hunger for ass that I couldn't manage to meet on my own. That had definitely been difficult for me in the past — first in the early stages of our relationship when I realised I couldn't keep up with his libido, then even more heartbreakingly, later on, when I realised that the man I loved had been cheating on me constantly for well over a year with a long line of strangers. For some couples that would have been the breaking point. Some men would have left when they found out they'd been betrayed. Some men would have left when

1

their husband, after apologising for that betrayal, admitted that he needed the freedom to fuck other men whenever he felt the need.

I wasn't that kind of guy though. And luckily this kind of life was ideal for both of us: him because it meant he could satisfy his need to seduce and fuck any man he needed to, and me because it met a need to be cuckolded that I'd never even known I had.

So we were good now; I'd learned to accept that he still loved me no matter who he fucked, and I'd grown to love how uncontrollably aroused I got from him being with other men. So he'd go out and have his fun whenever he felt like it, then he'd come home to me and he'd tell me exactly what happened while I rode his cock to an incredible orgasm.

And sometimes —though not nearly frequently enough — sometimes I'd get to deliver my husband to another man's house and wait outside in the car while they fucked. It was torture, waiting there in the car, imagining but not knowing what they were doing with each other. But it was fucking incredible. And two nights in the same week was a real treat.

Julian sat in the passenger seat, messaging on his phone.

"What's he like?" I asked.

"Hot. Ripped. Wanna see?"

He brought up a photo, and turned his phone towards me so I could see it. I couldn't study it closely because I had to focus on the road, but it was clear that the guy in the photo was attractive. He was shirtless - lean and toned. Brown hair, neatly cropped brown stubble, and piercing eyes.

"He's hung too. I saw a pic of his cock."

For a total top, Julian definitely appreciated a big cock. And for him to comment on it, it must be pretty big. I mean, mine's definitely bigger than average but I'd never heard him refer to me as 'hung' before.

I'd never been to this neighbourhood before; it was out towards the edge of town, about twenty minutes drive from our place. It was similar though: nice, respectable houses, generously sized with well-maintained front gardens.

"Left here. This is his street."

The houses on this street were bigger and flashier. Some of the houses were well set back from the road, hidden behind high gates or trees, while others were set close to the street with grand entranceways designed to make an impression. "You sure this is the right place?" I asked.

Julian checked his messages again. "Yeah. Number thirty."

I slowed down so we could check the letterbox numbers. Number thirty was like a lot of the others; a large gate barring the way to a long driveway lined with trees.

"Shit, this place is nice. Did you know this guy was loaded?" I asked.

"Nah, I had no idea." Julian seemed impressed. "Hey, maybe he'll have a spa we can fuck in."

"Do you want me to let you out here? Or drive you in?" Usually I'd just park up on the street, so the idea of going up the driveway to the front door threw me a bit. But it excited me at the same time, because it meant Julian's hookup would see me there and know his cuckold was waiting outside.

Julian told me, "I reckon you should drive me in." He shot me a grin. "That'd turn you on, right? Delivering me right to the front door?"

He knew me too well. I drove up to the gate, wound my window down, and pressed the intercom button.

Silence for a few seconds. Then a man's voice through the speaker. "Julian?"

Julian leaned over me to speak. "Yeah, that's me."

"Cool. Come on in." With a clunk the gates unlocked and slowly slid open for us.

The driveway was lined with mature trees of multiple varieties, some with leaves that were starting to turn golden for the autumn. The driveway wasn't long, and soon we saw the house in front of us. It was like a modern version of a

Frank Lloyd Wright prairie-style house: like a whole collection of different sized boxes, stacked side-by-side and on top of each other, each one topped off with a wide, flat roof that overhung the corners of the house as though it was kind of floating of its own accord. Warm wood and cold stone bricks, and rows of tall windows, some of which were illuminated in the twilight. It was only two stories, but it sprawled out like it had started growing organically out of the ground. It was huge, and beautiful.

The driveway ended in a loop by the front door. I pulled up to a stop, and surveyed the house.

"You're gonna wait here then?" Julian asked.

I nodded. "Have fun. I'll be out here when you're done."

Julian leaned in and kissed me. "You're the best. Have fun out here," he teased. Then he opened the door and jumped out of the car.

The door opened before Julian had walked the whole way up the path, and I saw the man from the photo on Julian's phone. He was dressed in gym gear - thigh length shorts and a muscle shirt. Even from this distance I could tell he was toned by the definition of his shoulders and arms.

The two of them talked for a second. Then, the guy looked over at me. For a second he seemed to study me, like he was sizing me up. Then the two of them went inside and shut the door behind them.

The first part, after he goes inside a guy's house, has always been the most intense bit for me. My imagination goes wild while I imagine what they're doing. I wonder whether they're having a drink, making small talk while they let the sexual tension build. Or getting straight down to it, ripping each other's clothes off as soon as they're inside the door. Julian's not much of a romantic, so he often just gets down to business like it's... well, business. He's charismatic though, and loves getting into conversations with new people. So if the guy was interesting they could end up yarning like old friends, either before or after they'd fucked.

It wasn't long before I was hard, imagining what they were up to inside that big house. I adjusted my cock in my pants, but I knew better than to play with it. I just sat, and wondered, and watched out for any sign of life through those rows of tall windows.

After half an hour I could safely assume that they'd definitely be at it by now, even if they'd waited and had a drink or something first.

I got out of the car and walked around a little to stretch my legs. Lights shone through some of the windows, but none of them gave away what was going on inside. I paced to the corner of the house, nonchalantly peering around the corner to see if I could get any hint of what room they were in and what they were doing. But nothing; a couple more lights on this side but still no sign of movement. I noticed that it was a big house though, stretching back even further than I'd expected from looking at it from the front. It looked like there might be a pool back there, behind some trees. This guy must be seriously loaded.

I strolled back past the car to the other end of the house. I couldn't see anything though, because there were rows of trees that blocked my view. I figured the bedroom must face out onto the back of the house; for a moment I contemplated exploring around the side of the house to see if I could catch a glimpse of them, but I quickly put it out of my mind. Julian would be pissed if he caught me, and the guy he was fucking would think I was a creep. So I wandered back to the car. I adjusted the hard-on in my pants and got back in.

As I sat there in silence, my imagination kept on taking me in all kinds of directions — like it always does in these situations. I pictured them together in the bedroom: that muscular guy on all fours, back arched, while Julian stood there fucking him from behind. I imagined Julian brushing aside the long blonde hair that would keep falling in front of his face as he pumped this guy's ass. I wondered if Julian was making that stranger moan. No, that was a given. I wondered *how loud* he was making that stranger moan.

As I sat there imagining the two of them, my dick kept getting harder. It was always agony, denying myself the pleasure of grabbing it and jerking myself off while I pictured them. But I was good at this now, and good at exhibiting restraint. I just had to be patient, and wait till he was done though so I could hear all about it. If I was lucky he'd still have some energy left — and another erection in him — so that when we got home I could ride his cock while he told me all about what he'd done with that man. If he was too spent I'd need to wait till tomorrow for that, but the upside was that the more spent he was tonight, the more hot the story was probably going to be when I eventually got to hear it.

Before I knew it, it had been over two hours. He'd usually be done by now; this guy must be a top notch fuck. I got out of the car and paced again because my butt was falling asleep. I got back in the car and turned the stereo on; as arousing as it was, there's only so much daydreaming you can do before you need something else to hold your attention. Besides, my cock was aching by now and I needed to think about something else for a bit to give it a chance to go soft again.

After two episodes of my podcast I turned the car engine on for a minute, because I was worried I was close to draining the batteries running the stereo for so long. Still no sign of Julian, and no messages on my phone. It had been over three hours now, and it was past eleven.

I gave it a while longer, and listened to another episode of my podcast. By the time I'd finished, I was starting to feel annoyed. It was going to be after midnight by the time we got home now. I was glad he was having fun and all, but he knew I was waiting and that I had an early start in the morning. I started to worry a little too; maybe they weren't fucking at all.

Maybe the hookup was violent. Maybe he was some rich psychopath who invited trade around so he could murder them and bury them in his huge garden.

I fought off the urge to message Julian. But by 11:45 I was over waiting. I grabbed my phone and wrote out a message.

I don't mean to nag you, but are you almost done?

I got out of the car and paced around outside again. Then I checked myself, and quickly got back in the car. I didn't want Julian to come outside right at that moment, and for it to seem like I was standing there tapping my foot. I was seriously starting to get concerned though.

Almost ten minutes later my phone lit up. I grabbed it like a flash and read the message from Julian:

Hey I'm going to stay here tonight ok?

What the fuck.

Julian knew the rules: no going raw, no relationships, and *no staying over.* For a second I just stared at the screen in absolute rage, all the things I wanted to say to him right now running through my head. First of all, of course he knew the answer was going to be no. Maybe if we'd talked about it first, worked through it together, I'd be a little more okay with exploring the idea. But springing it on me like that? And leaving me sitting in the car outside this stranger's house for almost four hours before he tried to send me home alone? No. Fucking. Way.

I started writing an angry reply, but I couldn't figure out quite what to say, or even where to start. I deleted message, tried another one, and then sat there for maybe ten minutes or so trying to get my words straight. The whole time I sat there, I was painfully aware that Julian hadn't sent a follow-up message. He hadn't realised he'd fucked up. He

7

hadn't just decided maybe it would be better to leave. He knew I was right outside and he hadn't bothered to come talk to me about it. He was in there, in bed with this stranger, and he intended to stay there the whole night.

What if they were already tucked up in bed, in each other's arms, talking to each other in low voices while they started to fall asleep?

When that thought struck me, I wasn't at all prepared for how horny it was going to make me. My dick instantly got rock hard thinking about them falling asleep together, and I wanted to cum so bad in that moment. That's what made me realise how to respond to Julian.

Ok. Night babe, have fun

I started up the car, turned the headlights on, and drove down the long driveway. I stopped at the gates, and they started to open for me automatically. As I waited, my phone went off again. The message just said:

Thx, luv u

I was so fucking hard for the entire twenty minutes or so that it took to get home. I jumped out of the car, ran up the path to my front door, and fumbled with my keys, desperate to get inside. As soon as I was inside with the front door closed behind me, I pulled my cock out and started jerking myself off furiously. It only took me a few seconds, and I shot a massive load all over the floor as I pictured the two of them falling asleep in each other's arms.

CHAPTER 2

I reached out, half asleep, expecting my hand to find Julian's warm body in the bed next to me. That's how I'd always begin the slow process of waking up: finding him, shuffling myself over to fit neatly against the shape of his body, then feeling his cock stir against me as he'd slowly start to wake. But today all I found was an empty bed. The confusion of that discovery jolted me awake, and that's when I remembered that I was alone. He hadn't come home last night. I'd left him to sleep in the arms of another man.

I reached immediately for my phone to see if he'd messaged. But there was nothing. For a moment I was angry at him for not messaging me goodnight, not apologising for breaking the rules we agreed, not checking in to see if I was okay after being cucked more extremely than I'd ever been before.

I wondered if he'd feel strange waking up next to someone else. I pictured him stirring, nuzzling up against the body next to him in the bed, becoming puzzled when his half-asleep brain registered that the body he was clinging to wasn't mine. I wondered if he'd feel bad about that. In my imagination he didn't, though. In my imagination he clung tight to the muscular body of his new fucktoy, rubbing the guy's chest and pressing his hardening cock up against his toned butt. Getting excited for another round.

I got hard from the thought of it. I spat into my hand and lubed up my cock with it. Then I lay there in bed, stroking it while I pictured them lazily making out as they woke up properly, Julian sliding his cock into the guy's hole and fucking him gently as he nuzzled his neck.

It didn't take me long to cum. As soon as I did, I was angry at him again.

The whole time I was getting ready for work I expected to get a message any second, but there was nothing. It wasn't till I was sitting on the train, tense with anger and worry, that I gave up waiting for him to message me and decided to make the first move.

I had no idea what to say. Even though I felt within my rights, I didn't want to come across angry. I didn't want to be that kind of boyfriend. I typed message after message, deleting each one because it wasn't quite right. Eventually I just went with:

Missed you. How was it?

I sat there staring at my phone, waiting for that little tick to fill in to show that he'd read my message, and for that little bubble full of dots to show that he was writing something back. I sat there staring at my screen for the rest of the train ride, but nothing happened. He hadn't even read it.

By lunchtime he still hadn't messaged me. As much as it killed me to be *that* guy, I couldn't help myself from sending another message as I sat in the break room eating my ramen.

Hey. You all good? Starting to worry because I haven't heard from you

I sat staring at the screen, but still nothing. He still hadn't even read my first message from this morning.

That whole afternoon I couldn't concentrate on anything. I'd keep trying to do some work, but five minutes later I'd find myself staring at my messages again, or just staring off into space while I imagined what they were doing. I was so hard under my desk that I contemplated sneaking off to the toilets to knock one out, but I knew I was too anxious to enjoy it if I did.

It was about three thirty when, having zoned out staring at my messages again, I saw the little 'read' tick change colour. My heart stopped for a second. Then a wave of relief washed over me so hard I could physically feel it. I sat there and waited to see what the reply would be.

But after ten minutes, there was still no reply.

Now I was pissed. I didn't know what had stopped him messaging me, or even checking his phone, up until now. But at least until now there had been a small chance he could have a legitimate reason for being MIA: his phone could have died, he could have dropped it in the toilet, who knows? But now I was a hundred percent sure that he'd seen my message, knew I was worried about him, and had made a deliberate decision not to put me out of my misery.

Fuck messaging him. I dialled his number and called it. Twelve rings, no answer. It eventually went to voicemail, and I hung up. Now I was fucking fuming.

Julian what the hell is up? Where are you? Why are you ignoring me?

As soon as I hit send I felt embarrassed at the type of husband I'd become. But I was so angry at him for ignoring me that I didn't know what else to do. I sat there for another few minutes staring at the screen, waiting for a reply, before throwing the phone down on my desk in rage and storming off to the convenience store at the bottom of my building to buy chocolate to comfort-eat.

When I got back to my desk I checked my phone again. There was a message. For the second time today my heart stopped. I fumbled with the phone passcode three times as I frantically tried to get to the message. When I finally got it, I found:

> *Hey babe, sorry, been way distracted. Having fun. Tell you all about it tonight. Luv u*

I was stunned that after the seismic shock he'd sent through our marriage with his actions over the last twenty-four hours, that was all he could bother saying to me. I was so angry at him, as well as angry at myself for how horny his indifference was making me.

I was livid all afternoon, but I didn't bother trying to message him. I'd save it for when he got home.

That night was his shift at the bar so I knew he wouldn't be home till about nine thirty. It meant that once I got home from work, I had a few hours to myself to storm around the house, stewing about his behaviour and picturing all the savage things I'd say to him when he finally got home. But by around quarter to ten he still wasn't home, and I was just about to call him again when my phone buzzed. I picked it up, and found it was a message from him.

> *Hey babe, I know this is a big ask but do you think it would be ok if I stayed at Callum's place again tonight?*

I couldn't believe how out-of-line Julian was being right now, breaking the rules for a second night in a row. In that instant I knew I'd made a massive mistake not putting my foot down last night, because I'd gone and made the rules seem optional. That needed to end now.

I dialled his number. It rang on the other end for a long time, long enough that I thought it was about to go to voice-mail. But eventually Julian answered.

"Hey. You saw my message?" I could tell by the tone of his voice that he knew I was mad, and knew he'd crossed a line. It was that tone he used when he knew I was about to tell him off.

"Yeah," I replied. "You're seriously thinking of going back? Two nights in a row?"

There was a long pause. "I'm still here, at his place. I haven't left yet. I called in sick to the bar."

"You ditched your shift? What the hell have you been doing this whole time?"

Julian laughed. "You'll find out when I get home." When he didn't get a response from me he obviously realised that his teasing wasn't helping, and he changed tack. "Babe, I know this is totally against the rules and I'm like, really, really grateful that you're being cool about it. I'm just having heaps of fun with him and I wanna keep going. You understand, right?"

"Okay." What the hell else was I supposed to say? I felt like I'd suddenly gotten in over my head.

"Really? You're all good? You're the fucking best, babe."

"Send me some pics though," I told him. "Or better yet, videos. Okay? I want to at least get to see some of the action."

Julian laughed down the other end of the phone. "That's the Nick I know and love. Okay, I'll ask Callum if he's okay with sharing a few pics or something. Keep your phone on you, okay?"

I agreed.

"Cool. I gotta go, okay babe? Love you heaps."

"Goodnight," I said to him. "Love you. Have fun fucking him. You'll be home tomorrow, right?"

Julian chuckled. "I'll be home when I'm all done. Bye!"

Before I could say anything in response to that — before I

could even pause to wonder what that meant — he'd hung up.

Sitting in my bed watching television on my laptop alone, I felt kind of dejected. But at the same time it turned me on so much thinking about the two of them fucking, and falling asleep together again. It turned me on even more when I thought about the fact they'd been at it all day, and that this guy had somehow managed to keep Julian so enthralled that he'd blown off work to stay with him.

After about twenty minutes my phone went off. I paused the show I was watching, and grabbed my phone. It was an image file. I felt that familiar rush in my chest, that empty feeling in my stomach, that electricity in my cock, when I saw what it was: a selfie of Julian's face, his mouth stretched around a massive cock, his eyes looking directly at the camera.

I was instantly hard. I couldn't believe the size of that cock; that guy was hung like a fucking donkey. I started to touch my cock while I looked straight at Julian's eyes staring back at me.

A minute later my phone buzzed again. This time it was a video. In it a hand rested on the back of Julian's head, holding it in place as that mighty cock pushed itself slowly in and out of his mouth. Right in, deep, all the way down his throat, making him gag. Then slowly pulling all the way out, a rope of saliva hanging on the tip as it withdrew from his mouth. Julian winked at the camera, then the video was over.

I played the video over and over, stroking my dick in awe at it. I hoped like crazy there was another one coming; I wanted to see Julian with his cock inside the guy's ass. But after ten minutes, there was nothing. Twenty minutes, and still nothing. The whole time I just watched that same fifteen second video on repeat, watching Julian take that giant cock in his mouth. By the time I realised there was no more photos or videos coming, it didn't matter because I was so close. I pulled up the first photo again, and jerked my dick furiously as I stared into Julian's eyes, his mouth full of another man's cock.

I shot ropes of cum across my chest, my heart racing and breath heaving. By the time I'd caught my breath I already felt embarrassed for being set off by what was probably just the prelude to the main event. I wiped up the cum, then went to sleep, knowing that for the second night in a row my husband would be falling asleep, spent, in the arms of another man.

I didn't hear from Julian at all the next day. And that night — his third away from me — Julian didn't even bother messaging to tell me he wasn't coming home. I sat up, anxiously waiting, hoping my phone would go off, but knowing deep down that it wasn't going to. I debated with myself about whether to message or call him, but I had no idea what I'd say. By this stage I wasn't angry at him anymore, but I was scared. The sick feeling in the pit of my stomach was telling me that I was losing my husband, and I had no idea what to do about it. The only thing that helped — the only thing I could think of at all — was to pull up that photo of him and jerk myself off, imagining I was right there looking him straight in the eyes as another man unloaded in his mouth.

CHAPTER 3

Those next few days were kind of like the early stages of a break-up. Suddenly I had to get used to doing everything alone, and it felt really weird. Going to sleep without him, and waking up in an empty bed, was the hardest. But there were other things, too. Not having him there to discuss what we'd eat for dinner. Having no one to kiss goodbye as I walked out the door in the morning. No one laughing with me when something funny happened on the television.

I kept telling myself it was fine. Julian was coming back, he'd given no indication that he wouldn't. This was just the next stage of my journey as a cuckold. I had to admit, as hard as it was to deal with, it was fucking hot thinking about the way he'd just ditched me to spend a week fucking his new buddy.

In my moments of weakness, when my insecurities got the better of me, I'd message him. I didn't want to nag, so it would always be something casual, nonchalant. *How's it going? Having fun?* That kind of thing. Sometimes I'd get a short, kind of uninterested reply a few hours later. But sometime's I'd get nothing at all.

He didn't send any more pics or videos either.

I wanked constantly. On the fifth night — or the sixth? — I played with my dildo, imagining it was Julian fucking me. It made me think about whether I'd ever get to feel him inside me again, and before I knew it I was crying while I fucked myself, alone in my bedroom.

On day eight I got a call from Stags, the bar Julian and I owned together. I didn't hear from them that often; I was more of a silent partner, while Julian was the hands-on one. He'd do the books, the ordering, all the management. He'd do a few duty manager shifts each week too, which he enjoyed. I liked it too, because whenever he worked the bar he'd end up getting laid and coming home to tell me about it afterwards; the name of the bar itself was a subtle reference to the fact that it was a source of guys for Julian to cuck me with. Sometimes I'd come in and sit there at the bar on my own, watching him flirt with the clientele while he mixed drinks.

Harry, the regular duty manager, had called to check if Julian was okay. "We've been worried about him," he told me. "He must be really sick to be out of action this long."

I was surprised. I knew he'd called in sick that second night, but I just figured he'd been back at work since then. But apparently he hadn't; other people had been covering his shifts, and they were running low on supplies that he hadn't been around to put in orders for. Harry was starting to get concerned.

I made excuses, told Harry that Julian was on the mend and that he'd be back at work soon. As soon as I was off the phone I hastily sent Julian a message:

You haven't been at work? Things need doing, Julian. People are worried

No reply.

Please, you need to come home now

It was almost eleven that night by the time he replied:

Sorry babe. I know, I've been so slack. I'll be home tomorrow

Finally.

That night I could barely sleep from the crazy combination of emotions. Relief he was coming home, mixed with dread over the conversation we'd have to have, mixed with the arousal from imagining how much more intense his sex with Callum would be that night, knowing that their affair would be over in the morning.

I spent a good hour or so the next morning getting myself ready for Julian — body hair trim, body lotion all over, and cleaning out my insides. And the whole morning I rehearsed in my head — and out loud — what I'd say to Julian when he finally came home.

But as soon as he walked through that door, I forgot every word of what I'd prepared.

At first he just stood there, and I looked up at him from where I was sat at the dining table. He looked different. His shaggy blonde hair still looked the same as it always did, but he was wearing clothes that I didn't recognise. Jeans that were a little tighter than usual. An expensive-looking sweater. Not just that though; there was something about his face, his manner, that seemed different to how I remembered him from little more than a week ago.

"Hey," he said to me, awkwardly.

"Hey," I replied, just as awkwardly.

He pulled out a chair and sat down at the table with me. "I guess you're pretty pissed at me right now."

I didn't say a word.

"I understand if you're upset. I was gone a long time. That can't have been easy."

"It wasn't." I tried to sound relaxed, but I could hear the anger in my own voice. "Easy, I mean. You broke the rules. You never gave me any choice about whether I was okay with it." I could feel myself choking up a little. "I didn't think you were ever going to come home."

Julian took my hand. "I was always going to come home. You're my husband, and I love you. That hasn't changed, you know."

I felt a tear trickle down my cheek and quickly wiped it away.

"Nick, I'm sorry I didn't communicate better. I'm sorry I got so distracted and ignored you the way I did." Julian paused. "But I'm not sorry I made the choice I did, to stay there with Callum. I had the most amazing time with him, it blew my fucking mind and I'm so glad I did it."

I nodded and shook away the tears before they set in properly. "I'm glad. Honestly, I am. I'm happy you had a good time with him." I was kicking myself for letting him off the hook so easy, but I couldn't help myself from asking him, "Can you tell me about it?"

Julian grinned, and I could tell from that grin that he knew he was off the hook. He knew he'd escaped a bollocking because his pushover cuck boyfriend just couldn't wait to find out all the details of what he'd been up to.

"Of course, babe. You know I'll always tell you how it went. That's the rules, right?" He got up, walked over to the sofa, and sat down. He leaned back, hands clasped together behind his head as I got down on my knees in front of him. "What do you want to know?"

"Everything. Start at the beginning."

Julian chuckled. He knew the routine by now. "Okay. So, he let me in, gave me a glass of whiskey. We chatted for a little bit, but not that long because the sexual tension was, like, extreme, right from the start. Then he took me up to the bedroom. Not the master bedroom, this other bedroom he has just for fucking in so he doesn't have to invite randoms into his own room. Man, his house is huge."

As he spoke I nuzzled his crotch with my mouth, over the fabric of his pants. I stopped for a moment to ask, "Then what?"

"We made out. Fuck, it was *good*." The way he said that, it was like he was reliving the moment in his head. It was so goddamn hot. I unbuckled his belt and undid the fly on his jeans while he kept retelling the story.

"We got naked. He is so fucking hot you wouldn't believe it, Nick, I swear! Like, fucking ripped. Not massively muscular, but toned all over - he has a personal trainer so he's fit as fuck. And he's hung like a giant too."

I finally got Julian's jeans unzipped, and pulled them down a little. I was surprised to find that underneath, rather than his usual trunks, Julian was wearing a pair of tight, crisp white briefs. They hugged the bulge of his cock and balls tightly, so I could see the outline of his head through the fabric even though he wasn't hard yet. I reacted involuntarily with a little gasp. "You're wearing briefs. You never wear underwear like this. You hate underwear like this, don't you?" It was such a small detail, but it really threw me. "Where did they come from?"

"I was there for over a week, babe. Did you think I'd just wear the same underwear the whole time?" He chuckled and added, "Not that I needed underwear most of the time."

I looked Julian up and down and then it dawned on me that he was wearing a completely new set of clothes, right down to new shoes and socks.

"Callum got me some clothes to wear while I was there," Julian explained. "He said he liked this kind of underwear on me. Makes my package look good, apparently. And my ass. You like?"

God it was hot, knowing that this stranger had convinced Julian to wear slutty-looking underwear for him, that he'd always refused to wear when I'd suggested it. I nodded enthusiastically, lifted the waistband, and reached under the fabric. His cock was still soft; I cupped it in my hand, then slowly drew it out of his briefs and started to stroke it.

Julian continued. "I sucked his cock. I could barely get the whole thing in my mouth, and it made me gag when it was about half way in," he laughed. "The first couple of times, anyway. His cock is beautiful. Uncut, leaks like mad when he gets turned on, and it tastes fucking incredible." At that I could feel Julian's cock start to thicken a little. I licked the tip of his shaft, then put the whole thing in my mouth, my tongue dancing across the head the way he likes it.

"He was kinda rough, kinda dominant. It was hot. He bit my neck, threw me around a little. Then he pinned me down, face down on the bed and he whispered in my ear, 'I'm gonna fuck you now.'"

That surprised me so much I almost gagged on his cock. I took my mouth off it and looked up at him. "What? He wanted to fuck you? What did you do?"

Julian grinned at me. "What do you think I did, babe?"

Surely not. He is strictly, one hundred percent, top. "What?"

"I begged him to fuck me. And he did. My fucking god did it hurt at first, that cock. I haven't had a cock in me for years and then to start with that monster! But fuck it was good, I've never been fucked like that before in my life."

I was so stunned I had no idea what to say. If it had been any other time I probably would have been a little irritated; I'd tried to get him to bottom for me a few times over the years with no success, but he'd given his ass up just like that to Callum the first time he asked. But I was way too horny to be upset about it. The thought of Julian's face, grimacing as the pain of that big cock turned into absolute pleasure, had me rock hard. I greedily put his cock back in my mouth and mumbled, "Keep going."

"That first fuck lasted for hours," he told me. "He was relentless. He fucked me in every way possible. I came so hard, without even touching myself. And he slowed down for a minute or two but didn't stop. I thought once I'd blown my load I'd be done, but it just felt so good I didn't want him to stop."

I couldn't believe what I was hearing. I was dying to tug on my cock but I knew I'd cum in a second if I touched myself right now. I wanted Julian to be inside me when I finally lost it and came. Julian's cock, though, while thickening a little, wasn't getting hard, so I couldn't ride him yet. I took it out of my mouth, and stroked it with my hand, my saliva providing the lube.

Julian could obviously sense my growing frustration. "It might take a bit of encouragement," he admitted, apologetically. "I already nutted this morning. With Callum."

"Did he fuck you again after that first time?" I asked him, stroking his cock.

"Of course. That's all we did. That whole time, I didn't fuck him once. He turned me into a bottom, I guess." That made him laugh. "He fucked me like, several times a day, every day. And he made me cum every time. There were a couple of points where I'd feel myself cum but nothing would come out, because he'd already fucked every last bit of it out of me. Drained me dry. It was such a fucking wild feeling.

"That first night, he woke up in the middle of the night and fucked me again. We fucked all night; I barely slept at all. Then like mid-morning he woke me up fucking me again, and we lay around in bed all day just chilling, making out. I thought I'd probably head home at some point, but then he told me to stay again. That night we moved from the fuck room into the master bedroom, and then that pretty much became our routine: wake, fuck, eat, chill, fuck, chill, eat, fuck, sleep. Repeat."

I could feel his cock suddenly start to get hard in my hand

as he told he how good it felt waking up next to Callum. "I'd be half asleep, and I'd feel his cock rubbing against my hole. And he'd nuzzle my neck, and I'd just back up onto him, and he'd fuck me gently till I was awake. Then rough till I came."

By now his cock was rock hard. I didn't waste any time. I scrambled to get my pants off, lubed up Julian's cock with my spit, and climbed onto him. As I felt his long shaft push its way into me I felt complete in a way I hadn't since the night he left. I bucked up and down, milking his cock with my ass. "Fuck, bae, it's so hot. I can't believe you let him fuck you!"

"I know. It was unbelievable. So good."

I kissed him. He kissed me back for a second before pulling away. "You know the hottest thing?" he asked. "He has these piercing eyes, and when he'd feel me getting close he'd get so close to me I could feel his breath, and he'd look into my fucking soul when I came on his cock."

God that was hot. In all the years together I'd never heard him talk like that.

"He fucking owned me. I spent that whole week just begging for him to fuck me, wandering around his mansion with his cum leaking out of me the whole time."

That admission made me reel. And the way Julian's eyes suddenly widened revealed that he'd just realised he'd said too much.

"You let him cum inside you?"

He said nothing for a second. And that second was all it took; the thought of Julian having another man cum inside him, over and over, was enough to set me off instantly. I felt the rush through my balls and my cock, and I felt my dick contract and pulse as it erupted. I wailed in pleasure, embarrassment and dismay as my dick convulsed and shot wads of cum into the air and onto Julian's new sweater. My breath heaved, and for a several seconds I couldn't say anything at all.

Julian breathed a sigh of relief. "Oh thank fuck," he said.

"I thought you were gonna be upset that we didn't use condoms." He paused, then admitted, "You know, I've got his load in me right now."

Part of me thought I should yell at him. But it was too late: my body had already given away how I really felt, and the way my spent dick pulsed again when he said that just confirmed it. I lifted myself off his cock and flopped down onto the sofa next to him. In that moment I didn't know what to do. He'd broken one of the basic covenants of our relationship — *another* of the basic covenants. And I knew by letting myself show how much it turned me on, I'd just given him tacit permission to keep doing it.

I started to stroke his cock again, but he brushed my hand aside. "Hey, I'm okay," he said. "Like I said, I've cum already today." He leaned over and kissed me. "Thanks for being cool with this. I know it must have been pretty intense."

"Thanks." There was an awkward silence, which I broke by asking him, "So, do you think you'll want to go back for a repeat some time?"

"Oh yeah, Callum's back a week Monday so I'm gonna go over then." He awkwardly added, "If it's okay by you," as an afterthought.

"Back?"

"Yeah, he went to New York this morning on business."

"This morning?" My heart sank because I instantly realised what that meant. "So if he hadn't gone to New York, would you even have come home?"

Julian paused for just a tiny bit too long, and when he tried to assure me, "Sure, babe," it was entirely unconvincing. He knew it too, so he gave up the pretence; he just sighed and said, "Babe, I'm back now. That's all that matters."

We sat in silence for a minute. My heart was stinging from the feeling of being relegated to second-best, and still racing from the orgasm I'd just had. I felt so satisfied, but at the same time I could feel the tears coming and I desperately wanted them not to. Finally, I put on my best cheerful voice and asked, "So, now that you're a bottom, does that mean I can fuck you some time?"

Julian just chuckled and shook his head. "Nah, I'm good thanks."

CHAPTER 4

When Callum cut his trip short, Julian didn't waste any time. He didn't even ask whether I was okay with it, he just told me that he was going back to his place to spend the night. He promised that it was only for one night though, "Because Callum has to go to Tokyo tomorrow anyway." He also promised I could drop him off and pick him up.

I thought I'd be angry, but to be honest I was too horny for that. I could feel my dick get hard as I drove up Callum's driveway and pulled up outside the house. Julian gave me a kiss on the cheek and jumped out, almost running up to the front door. As soon as it opened he flung his arms around Callum and kissed him. Callum's hands found their way onto Julian's butt as they stood there in the doorway making out for what seemed like a good minute or two. Then Callum motioned for Julian to step inside. As he did, Callum looked over at me, impassively, not giving away even an inkling of what was going on in his head. Then the door closed, and Julian belonged to Callum again for the night.

I went home, and spent over an hour edging myself, imagining them fucking till Julian, exhausted, fell asleep in Callum's arms.

The next morning as I was getting ready to pick him up, I got a text from Julian:

Hey babe, Callum's trip got cancelled so I'm going to stay a few extra days. I'll let you know when to come get me.

I should have seen that coming. I considered texting back demanding that he came home, or just telling him how pissed off I was. But as I thought about what to say, and how disrespectful he was being, it just made me hard. So instead of picking a fight, I sat at home jerking off at the thought of how Julian had just ditched me again.

It was another five nights before he finally gave me the okay to come collect him. *But not till late this afternoon,* he told me. *We want to spend the day together.*

So I was there at four o'clock, sitting in my car waiting for them. They knew I was there — Callum had to let me in the security gates — but they still took their time. Finally though, the door opened and Julian stepped out. He gave me a casual wave and a nod to acknowledge me, and then he turned, said something to Callum, and kissed him goodbye.

At least I thought he was kissing him goodbye. They started to make out, gently, but then gaining in intensity. Callum grabbed Julian, one hand on his ass and one in the small of his back. Julian reached down and started fondling Callum's crotch. And the next thing I knew, Julian had his other hand on Callum's chest, gently pushing him back into the house. Then they were gone, and the door shut behind them.

For fuck's sake.

For about half an hour I sat in the car, not sure how long they'd be but absolutely sure what they were doing inside. I knew that messaging Julian to hurry him up wasn't an option, I just had to be patient and wait till they were done. Even if it meant losing the rest of my afternoon. To be honest, I'd rather be sitting there in my car outside Callum's house with am erection than just about anywhere else.

After an hour though, I figured it was getting ridiculous. Against my better judgement I picked up my phone and dialled Julian's number. It rang, and rang, but there was no answer. I wondered whether he just didn't notice it ring, or whether he'd chosen to ignore it. The thought made my dick even harder; fuck, I needed Julian to finish soon because I wasn't sure how much longer I could go without jerking myself off to completion.

But pretty soon I got my answer: my phone lit up with a message:

I'm going to stay, come get me tomorrow.

So with a frustrated sigh I started up the car and headed back down the driveway, headed for another night at home alone getting myself off to the thoughts of my pitiful situation.

———

The following day when I showed up, Julian didn't keep me waiting. Callum didn't come to the door with him, so they must have said their goodbyes already. When Julian climbed into the car he seemed to be almost floating.

Before he could say anything I let loose; I was pissed, and hurt, about what he'd done yesterday. "That was an asshole move yesterday. You had me come all the way over, sit in my car for over an hour, and then basically just told me to fuck off again."

Julian looked a little guilty. A little, but not very. "Sorry babe. I just lost track of time. You loved it though, sitting out there waiting for us to finish, right?"

He knew me way too well. It was hard to berate him when he was a hundred percent right.

"How was it?" I asked him.

"Fuck, it was good," he told me. "God, I wish someone had shown me years ago that being fucked could feel that good."

Julian leaned over. "Babe," he whispered in my ear, "I'm full of his cum. Maybe I'll let you eat it out of me when we get home."

My cock was instantly throbbing, and my heart followed suit, so loud I could hear it thumping in my ears. It was almost impossible to concentrate on driving, and I must have driven like a maniac in my enthusiasm to get home. The whole time, all I could think about was Callum's seed slowly leaking out of Julian, and how much I needed to taste it before any more of it was lost.

As soon as we got in the driveway I was out of the car and up to the front door, fumbling frantically with the keys while Julian sauntered casually behind me. Once we were inside I grabbed his hand and almost dragged him to the bedroom. "Get on all fours," I ordered, the desperation in my voice clear to both of us.

Julian obliged, and as soon as he was on the bed on all fours I pulled down his joggers. God damn, there was already a dark, wet patch in his briefs where the cum had leaked out and soaked through them. Seeing that made my own dick leak a little too. I put my nose up to it and inhaled the scent of Callum's cum. It made my head spin.

I slowly peeled down Julian's underwear, revealing his freshly fucked ass. Julian didn't have much hair around his ass crack, but what he did have was slick with semen. His hole was loose, pink, freshly fucked open. I couldn't believe this was happening, couldn't believe that I was actually staring at the wrecked asshole of my usually-exclusively top boyfriend.

I tentatively licked around his hole. I could taste it immediately; it was musky and salty and sweet. I teased Julian's hole with the tip of my tongue. He reacted instantly, letting out a sigh of pleasure. He relaxed into it, and as he did his hole twitched, releasing a thread of semen that ran down his ball sack. I quickly lapped it up before it could disappear - my first mouthful of Callum's cum. It felt gelatinous as it slid down my throat. I felt a dribble of precum release itself from my cock, only to be absorbed into the fabric of my underpants.

I pushed my tongue into Julian's hole. He let out a little moan.

"Do you like that, bae?" I asked.

"Yeah, it's good. My hole's so fucking sore, your tongue's such a relief."

I licked down his taint to his balls, and then back up to his hole. "Tell me what he did to you," I asked, before I plunged my tongue deep into his hole, making him gasp.

"Fuck, babe!" It took him a second to relax into it again, and as soon as he did I tasted more of Callum's sweet cum on my tongue. "You want to know what he did to me?"

I mumbled a yes, without taking my tongue out of his ass.

"He lay me down on the bed and held me real tight," Julian told me. "He got me to wrap my legs around him, and he fucked me real slow, real gently. With his arms around me real tight, and his chest pressing down on mine so I couldn't move even if I wanted to."

I could picture it as I licked and suckled at his hole. It made me go harder, trying to get all the cum out that I could. I reached around to touch his cock, but he gently batted my hand away.

"Every time he thrust into me his torso kinda massaged my cock," he went on. "He made me cum that way, then he just kept fucking me till I got hard again."

I took a break from the inside of his hole to run my tongue

up and down his cum-slick ass crack, before diving deep in again.

"Then he put me on my knees like I am right now. On the edge of the bed so he could stand. And he pounded my ass so hard, fuck, I thought he was gonna break me." The wistfulness in his voice told me that he was reliving it his mind right now, even while I was there servicing him. That made my dick throb. By now my groin felt wet from the amount of precum I was leaking.

"He held me by the hips and slammed me hard till my knees gave out."

"Then he came in your ass?"

"He'd already busted inside me once already by that stage. But he always just manages to keep going without barely even stopping. I was a sloppy mess by that stage. But yeah, he came inside me again."

"How many loads did he put in you?" I stopped long enough to ask.

"Two last night, two this morning."

I couldn't help myself by this point; I slowly reached into my pants and started jerking my dick as I ate him out. "That's so hot," I admitted.

"When he gave me the last load this morning, you know what he said?"

I mumbled, "What?"

"He said he wanted to make sure I was full of his seed so I wouldn't forget my ass belongs to him."

That did it; I'd only been stroking for a few seconds but when I heard him say that I felt the familiar swell of an unstoppable orgasm. With a little gasp I felt a wad of cum release itself into my underwear. I jerked my cock a few more times to get the rest out, then collapsed onto the bed.

Julian saw I was done, and he pulled his pants back up, as though he'd just been waiting impatiently for me to finish.

"You like tasting his cum on me?" he asked as he got up and tied up the drawstrings on his joggers.

I licked my lips and tasted the salty sweetness again. "Fuck yes," I admitted. "I want him to cum in you again."

"That's lucky. Because he's back in town on Wednesday so I'm going back. He's got nowhere to go for a while so I'll probably stay a week or so this time."

"Again?" I asked. "You're over there basically all the time now, except for when he's away."

"Of course," he replied, as though he didn't even register anything out of the ordinary about it. "There's nowhere I'd rather be."

————

I tried to set down some ground rules for the next visit, with limited success. Julian wouldn't agree to send me photos or video of him and Callum having sex, because he said that Callum wasn't really into it. He did promise, however, that from now on he'd make sure Callum put a load in him just before he left, and that I'd be allowed to lick it out of him when he got home. He also promised that he wouldn't flake on his shifts at the bar while he was staying with Callum. He made it very clear, however, that he would be staying there for several days at a time — frequently — and that I wasn't to complain or beg him to come home.

I agreed to everything. Hearing him make those demands, and so few concessions to accommodate my feelings, made me a little sad. The whole situation made me terrified, too, that this was all going too fast and I was headed towards losing him. But my body couldn't lie about the fact that the whole situation made me crazy horny. It was the stuff of all my fantasies, even the ones I thought were too extreme to come true.

The night Callum was back in town I offered to drop

Julian off at his house again. After checking with Callum though, Julian told me that tonight would be a little different. "He's taking me on a date," he said. "So if you want you can drop me off."

"A date?" I was taken aback by that suggestion. Even though they'd already been hanging out fucking for days on end, the idea of the two of them going on a date seemed to be crossing another line and taking things a whole step further. Julian had already broken two of our rules — no fucking raw, and no staying over — and now it sounded like he was steadily headed towards breaking the one remaining rule: no relationships. "I don't know if I like the idea of you going on a date with him."

Julian looked a little confused, and maybe a little annoyed. "What do you mean? We hang out and eat together all the time at his place. What's the difference if we go out somewhere?"

Surely he could see why it was different. "It seems like more than just sex."

Julian laughed. "Of course it's more than just sex, babe," he replied. "I thought that was kind of obvious by now."

The reaction on my face must have been clear, because Julian stopped smiling. He took a step closer, gently put his hands on my arms and looked straight in my eyes. "Don't worry, babe. Just try to focus on how much it turns you on, okay? I know it must be kinda scary, how fast things are changing." He paused, like he wasn't sure how much he should say. "Callum and I, we've had dates already, you know. Like we've hung out and talked for hours, eaten dinner together, done romantic stuff. It's just that it's mostly been at his place till now. He wants to take me out somewhere nice, show me a good time."

"You remember the rules we set right at the start of all this, right?" I asked. "No going raw, no staying over, and no relationships."

Julian looked a little confused. "Yeah, of course I remember. I just figured it was kind of obvious those rules don't apply with Callum. You were fine with me staying over, you were more than fine with him putting loads in my ass. Am I right?"

I nodded; I had to agree with that.

"And I want a relationship with Callum. I mean, hell, I already have a relationship with him. But I want to take it as far as we can."

I'm losing him. I could feel the tears welling up at the same time I could feel my dick swelling, thinking of Julian falling in love with Callum and forgetting about me.

"I know that's hard to handle," he continued. "But we both know you love being a cuck. You can enjoy this if you want to — the only reason you're not is that you think you're not supposed to. You think you're supposed to be the only man I care about."

I was no longer the only man Julian cared about. That thought made me so sad, but turned me on so much.

Julian looked me dead in the eyes, hands on my shoulders. "I want to know you're okay with this. Are you okay with this?"

I relented. Of course I did. "I want you and him to be together." Even though it was true it scared me so fucking much to say it. I held back the tears from breaking and washing down my face. "Go get ready. I'll drop you off for your date."

I drove him to *Trophé*, an upscale restaurant on the waterfront downtown. I'd wanted to go there ever since it had opened a few months earlier, but had never had an occasion special enough to justify the expense. The expense probably wasn't even something Callum noticed though.

Julian was dressed in slim-fitting trousers that hugged the shape of his ass, and a silk shirt — one he never wore unless he was trying to impress — unbuttoned to half way down his chest. Julian looked good no matter what he wore, but even so, I couldn't help noticing that he never dressed up like that for me.

I could tell Julian was excited, and a little nervous. When I pulled over outside the restaurant he checked himself in the mirror and adjusted his hair. Then he turned to me. "Thanks for the lift, babe. And thanks for being cool with this." He gave me a chaste kiss on the cheek, and got out of the car.

As he walked away into the restaurant, I couldn't help noticing how great his ass looked. It made me think to myself that I was a fucking idiot for letting such a perfect guy fall for another man. But that thought just turned me on.

I drove home, and masturbated to the thought of them sharing a romantic date. After blowing a huge load I watched television till I fell asleep. I didn't hear from Julian that night, or the next, or the next.

Over the days that followed I fell back into what was fast becoming my new life — one of celibate bachelorhood, each night a combination of sitting in front of the television on my own, and masturbating to fantasies of what my husband was doing without me. By day five it felt relatively normal living this life on my own. I kept telling myself Julian would be back any day now. But honestly, part of me thought that maybe he'd forgotten I existed. Thinking about that made me feel a little sick, but it also made me cum hard, every single time.

CHAPTER 5

I was surprised when Julian finally said I could meet Callum in person. I'd dropped hints, and even asked outright a couple of times, but Julian had always ignored my requests. The one time I'd pinned him down about it he'd just told me matter-of-factly that Callum had no interest in meeting me, so I should probably just leave it alone.

So it had come as total surprise when Julian told me I should come meet Callum for a drink. I'd asked what had changed, and Julian just told me "I guess Callum was curious after all."

Things were definitely starting to get serious between the two of them. After the night I'd dropped Julian at the restaurant for their date, he'd stayed over at Callum's place for more than a week. Since then he'd been back there twice more: first for another week, and then for an agonising, seemingly endless ten days. Basically whenever Callum wasn't out of town, Julian was around at his place.

Whenever Julian went to stay with Callum I'd hear virtually nothing from him. He'd vanish from my life entirely, only to turn up without warning and with Callum's fresh load in his ass. He stopped fucking me entirely; my only sexual contact with him was when I'd greedily eat Callum's loads out of him when he'd return home from his stays. I missed being fucked, and I missed feeling like I was the most important person in Julian's life. But I was happy for him that he was sexually fulfilled. And as hard as it was to deal with, it was so goddamn hot knowing he was getting loaded up by his bull day in, day out.

But as hot as it was knowing that Julian was spending his time with another man, I longed to actually see them together, to be closer to the action. So I was relieved and excited when Julian suggested I should come and meet Callum for a drink.

"Come down to the bar on Friday," Julian suggested. "We'll be there anyway."

That surprised me. "You're going to take him down to Stags? With everyone we know?"

"Oh yeah, he comes down there all the time. Like when I'm on the bar, or after work. Most of the guys have hung out with him already."

I could feel my face go red with the embarrassment of it. A whole bunch of my friends had met this guy before me. And none of them had even said anything to me about it. What the hell must they think of me?

Julian went to stay at Callum's on Tuesday night, so by the time Friday rolled around, I hadn't seen him for a while. I was so excited, and so shit-scared, to finally meet the new man in Callum's life, that I was trembling like an addict in withdrawal while I got ready. I tried on about five different shirts, my shaky hands fumbling with the buttons each time, until I finally found one that I thought I looked decent enough in that I could cut it with a guy like Callum.

When I got down to the bar, about eight thirty, I was initially too nervous to even go inside. I stood out on the street, pacing, until I finally summoned up the balls to walk in. When I pushed open the door I saw them immediately. Julian and Callum were sitting close together in a booth, surrounded by three or four other guys. Two of them I recognised: our friends Josh and Davey. The others I couldn't see because they were facing away from me.

I slowly walked over to them. Callum glanced in my direction but gave no indication that he recognised me. I didn't know if that was some kind of power play or something he was doing for a laugh — pretending like I wasn't memorable enough — or if he literally didn't remember what I looked like. As I got closer to the table I desperately hoped that Julian or one of the guys would recognise me, acknowledge me, welcome me over. But instead as I got closer I felt like I was intruding on a closed conversation — an unwelcome interloper, even though I literally owned the whole fucking bar.

I stopped awkwardly at the full table, and waited for a gap in the conversation. After a second Callum looked up at me again, impassively, like he was expecting me to take his drink order. A couple of seconds later Julian finally noticed me. "Babe, you're here!" He didn't get up. Davey did though; he hugged me and said hi. Josh was trapped in the booth so didn't get up, but he greeted me cheerfully.

I barely noticed them though. I couldn't take my eyes off Callum. It was so strange, finally seeing him close up like this. After him just being a photo, or a figure seen fleetingly from a distance. He had a frame that was lean but obviously muscular - I could tell by the way his tee clung to his shoulders and chest, but hung loosely off his lower torso. He was stunningly handsome; he had a long face with a strong, angular jaw that was dusted with stubble. His hair was neatly cropped on the sides, and longer on top; styled in a way that looked both flawlessly manicured and effortless at the same time. And he had thick eyebrows, which looked permanently furrowed in thought in a way that added to the intensity of his electric-blue eyes. Those eyes fixed on me, giving nothing away.

Julian introduced him. "Nick, this is Callum. Callum, Nick."

Callum stood up, and extended his hand. "Nick." He seemed to be studying me closely.

"Hi, I'm Nick," I stammered pointlessly. I took his hand. His grip was strong, but not like he was trying to make a point of it. He didn't take his eyes off mine for the duration of what seemed like the longest handshake in the world. "Nice to meet you finally. I've heard so much about you," I told him with a nervous laugh.

"I bet you have." The corner of his mouth turned up in a cocky half-smile.

He sat down and gestured to the extra seat that Davey had pulled over from another table for me to sit on. "Oh, I'll just grab a drink first." I was desperate to get away for a second and compose myself before I completely freaked out. "Anyone need anything?"

"Champagne and two APAs," Callum said, with an authority in his voice that made it clear it was an instruction and not a request.

"Yes sir," I said, without thinking. As soon as I said it, I realised how pathetic I sounded. I caught Josh sniggering, and I felt my face flush with humiliation. I turned and bolted for the bar.

Harry was on the bar tonight. He was one of our longest employees, and a good friend. He greeted me enthusiastically: "Nick! Long time no see. How you been, dude?"

"Hey man, I've been okay," I told him. "One champagne, two APAs and a cider, thanks Harry."

As he poured the drinks Harry looked at me suspiciously, then over at the table, then back at me. He looked like he wanted to say something but was hesitating, until he eventually just decided to go for it. He gestured with his chin towards Julian and Callum's table. "That can't be easy, seeing Julian get close with him like that."

I shook my head. "What are you talking about? You know what our relationship's like." If anyone should know, it's Harry. He'd seen Julian in action picking up guys at the bar every week, and he'd been fucked dozens of times by Julian over the years himself.

Harry seemed unconvinced. "You know it's not just sex, right? They're like a legit couple. Julian introduces Callum to people as his boyfriend."

I pretended to look like I wasn't shocked, but inside I was reeling. I felt a hint of panic rising up in me as I contemplated the prospect that I'd been replaced. At the same time though, I felt my dick thickening, and I desperately hoped I wasn't going to get an erection here at the bar where everyone could see.

"It's fine," I said, a little more defensively than I'd intended. I grabbed my drinks and walked away without another word.

The rowdy conversation at the table subsided a little as I approached with the drinks. I sat down and handed out the drinks; the champagne was for Callum, and the beers were for Julian and some guy I'd never met before. As I handed him the glass the guy introduced himself: "Hey man, thanks for the drink. I'm Dale. You a friend of Julian's then?"

I looked at Julian and Callum as an awkward silence descended on the table, wishing someone would step in so I didn't have to explain the situation. Julian and Callum both just looked at me, saying nothing. So eventually I replied to Dale, "I'm Julian's husband."

Dale looked confused. He looked at the couple, pressed up against each other, Julian's hand resting on Callum's thigh. "But…" He looked like he was trying to calculate where he'd misunderstood.

Callum stepped in. "I'm fucking Nick's husband," he explained.

"Oh," Dale didn't look any less confused; he looked at me

for confirmation. I just nodded. I could feel my face burning with the humiliation.

With that awkward moment over, the conversation around the table resumed as though nothing had happened. A couple of the other strangers introduced themselves to me, but then largely ignored me after that. Callum and Julian were both so charismatic and entertaining that they basically held the attention of the table all evening.

At one point Josh leaned over and quietly said to me, "You must be loving this, huh Nick? I mean, this must be taking your cuckold fetish to a whole new level!"

I mumbled my agreement, but I was too absorbed hanging off all Callum's words to really engage.

"He's fucking handsome, right?" Josh continued.

"Yeah," I agreed, studying his sapphire eyes and his magnetic smile from across the table.

"And a really awesome guy too. So smart, and funny. And successful. And fucking loaded! God, I'm jealous of Julian! Every time we hang out I kinda want to try steal him for myself, haha."

I wondered if all my other friends felt the same way. They were bound to, Callum was superior to me in basically every way. I felt like such a loser, watching as my husband paraded around his new, better partner and all our friends lapped it up.

Every now and then I'd try to insert myself into the conversation. But whenever I'd try to say something witty or interesting it would fall flat. Occasionally Callum would give me a smirk, as if he was enjoying seeing me try and fail to get a word in at a table of my own husband and friends. But mostly no one noticed me at all. Callum and Julian were the centre of attention, and loving it. They hung off each other, touching each other as they talked, sharing intimate whispers just between the two of them, and kissing each other tenderly like a couple in love.

Gradually the bar started to fill up with the Friday night crowd. Various people would wander up to the table to greet the two of them and chat. I was surprised just how many of the regulars — my friends — seemed to already know Callum, and know the two of them as a couple. They'd converse with the familiarity of old friends, then they'd notice me and suddenly be unsure how to react. With each of my friends that came over, I'd see that moment of guilt where they realised they'd so completely accepted Callum and Julian as a couple that they'd all but forgotten I existed. Seeing me there was an uncomfortable reminder.

At one point I got up to get us more drinks — that had somehow ended up being my job all night, without either of them having to even ask — and I came back to find the booth vacated. I looked around and found the whole group on the dance floor, Callum and Julian grinding against each other and making out. Seeing them like that made both my dick and my heart ache; it was such a mindfuck to feel so rejected and so fucking horny at the same time.

The two of them could barely keep their hands off each other, they were virtually fucking on the dance floor, albeit still fully clothed. So it was no surprise when, after a few minutes, Julian led Callum off the dance floor and the two of them headed towards the door. It hurt my heart to see that it didn't look like Julian was going to even bother saying good-bye. I argued with myself inside my head about whether I should go over and try to talk to them before they left. Eventually I decided I would. I'd look like a desperate idiot, for sure, but that ship had sailed long ago.

I walked over as they were putting their coats on. "You guys going already?"

"Hey babe!" Julian replied, as though he'd only just realised I was even here. He sounded tipsy. "Yeah, we're going back to Callum's. We both need to fuck, like, now."

I looked at Callum. He just looked back at me like my existence bored him.

"Hey, you could come back to our place if you want," I suggested, trying to sound nonchalant but knowing I came across desperate. "It's closer, you know."

Julian looked at Callum for approval. For a second he gave nothing, but then that arrogant smirk spread across his face and he replied, "Yeah, sure." The two of them turned around and walked out of the bar. I hurriedly grabbed my coat and ran after them.

They walked out to a black Tesla Model 3 that was parked up outside the bar, and a tall, handsome guy in a slim-fitting black suit got out. The guy opened the back doors of the car for Julian and Callum, and they climbed in. I just stood there, not sure whether to try get in with them, suddenly not even sure if I had their permission to ride home with them. I could tell that Callum had noticed me standing there, expectantly, but he wasn't doing anything to help. The asshole wanted to make it as awkward for me as possible. Eventually I kind of stammered, "Should I…?" and gestured to the front passenger door. The driver turned and looked at me, then looked back at Callum for direction.

Callum waited just a beat, just to make it that much more awkward. "Front passenger seat," he said, when he'd made me wait long enough.

The drive home was one of the most awkward experiences of my life. Julian and Callum were all over each other, slowly unbuttoning each other's shirts as they made out in the back of the car, while the driver and I sat in silence. I could hear the blissful sighs, and the wet noise of their kisses, and I strained to see as much as I could through the rear view mirror without making it obvious I was looking. Listening to them go at it made me start to get hard, and I prayed like hell that Callum's driver couldn't see the tent starting to form in my pants.

When we finally pulled up in front of the house the two of them stumbled out of the car and up the path to the front door. I trailed behind, watching them fumble as they tried to navigate while continuing to make out the entire time. At the front door Julian patted himself down, before eventually realising that he didn't even have a key to the house with him. The two of them waited for me to unlock the front door. Julian then took Callum by the hand and led him into our house for the first time.

I watched as Callum surveyed the living room. "Welcome to my house," Julian said to him. "Want me to show you around?"

Callum pulled him close and kissed him. When he was done he released him and replied, "Sure. Show me your place."

I followed as Julian led Callum by the hand into the kitchen. That's about as far as the tour got; within a couple of seconds Callum had Julian pinned up against the kitchen counter, pressing against him and kissing him forcefully. The counter was dotted with stuff, but in a single gesture Callum swept everything off the counter and onto the floor, lifting Julian up and sitting him on the edge of the counter. The bottle of wine smashed on the floor, red wine and broken glass everywhere. The same with the fruit bowl my mother had given me as a gift; it smashed on the floor and the fruit rolled across the artificial floorboards. Neither of them seemed to notice, they were too absorbed in each other as they kissed, Julian's legs wrapped around Callum's waist and his arms around Callum's neck.

For a while I just stood there and watched. I'd never seen someone manoeuvre Julian so confidently and forcefully. Julian was a completely different man with Callum; he was swept up in a kind of passion that I don't think I'd ever provided for him. Julian moaned breathlessly as Callum kissed his neck. His arms flailed around, knocking more things off the countertop as he tried to find something to clench onto.

After a while they came up for breath. "Hey, get me a drink," Callum ordered, not bothering to look at me.

I snapped to it. "Would you like a beer?" I offered. "Wine?"

"Wine." Then he thought about it for a second. "No, whiskey. You got any whiskey?"

"I'll check." The liquor cabinet was right there behind me, so I turned and started to hurriedly rummage around in it, desperate to not miss a second of watching them together. I grabbed the whiskey, then I quickly found my set of rarely used crystal whiskey tumblers and grabbed one for each of us.

I turned around, to find Julian rubbing Callum's cock through his pants, his shirt fully unbuttoned now, and Callum kissing his chest. I didn't want to interrupt this moment. But I also didn't want to keep Callum waiting. I nervously cleared my throat. "Um, do you want ice in it?" I asked.

They stopped kissing. Callum looked around at me, his hands still resting on Julian's thighs. "Nah, neat is good." He reached out and I handed him the glass. I also put one carefully down on the counter next to Julian's hand.

Callum necked the shot of whiskey in one gulp. Then he grimaced and looked at me angrily. "God, what the fuck was that bullshit?" he asked.

I was confused. "It's whiskey." That's what he'd asked for, I was sure of it.

"Do you brew this in your fucking bathtub or something? It's fucking vile." He picked up Julian's glass, telling him, "I don't want you to have to drink this shit." With that, he casually tossed the two glasses aside. When they hit the floor they smashed into hundreds of tiny pieces, the crystal sparkling golden from the residue of the whiskey inside them.

"I'm going to piss. Find me something decent to drink," he ordered.

Once he was out of the room there was a long moment as I just looked at Julian incredulously. "What the hell?" I asked, finally.

Julian just laughed. "He likes top shelf, dude."

"He's an asshole. Did you see what he did to my crystal glasses?"

That made Julian laugh again. "What can I say? He does what he likes, he's hard to control. That's part of what turns me on about him. That energy, that's what makes me want to give my ass up to him every time he wants it."

I paused, not knowing if I wanted to have this conversation right now. But I couldn't not, so I went for it: "Harry said you call him your boyfriend. In front of everyone we know."

"Well he is my boyfriend," Julian replied, irritated. "I told you, I want to take it as far as I can with him. A real relationship. And you said you were okay with it."

"Yeah, but—"

"But what?"

"But I didn't realise I'd be humiliated like that in front of everyone."

"You love it though."

He was right. Fuck, it hurt but it was so arousing, the feeling of being completely humiliated in front of everyone I knew.

"Look," Julian said. "You can't go trying to police my relationship with him, set all these rules that I don't even know exist. You don't get to make rules about my relationship with him. We'll do what we want."

I had nothing to say in response to that. I realised I'd been stupid to expect I'd have any control over the situation from here on in.

Julian changed the subject. "How 'bout we crack open that bottle of red that Vince and Rueben gave us?"

"Julian, that was a wedding gift. We're supposed to be saving it, you know? For a special occasion."

"Tonight is special." I hadn't even heard Callum come back into the room behind me. "First time you get to see what a real man does to your husband. And the night you get put in your place. Get the wine, okay?"

He beckoned to Julian and the two of them headed back into the living room. I located the wine and poured two glasses. I wondered whether it would seem strange that I didn't pour myself one. But I figured that any pretence that I wasn't pathetic was long gone. And I wanted to make sure they had as much as they wanted; even though it was my wedding present, it seemed kind of selfish for me to drink any of it myself.

When I came into the living room, Callum and Julian were sitting close together on the sofa, drunk-whispering and giggling as they nuzzled each other's necks. I nervously handed them the wine. Callum took his without acknowledging me or even looking at me, as though I was just a waiter at a cocktail party. I waited in nervous silence as he took a drink, but luckily this time it seemed to meet with his approval. The two of them continued to talk, ignoring me the whole time.

Callum pointed to the painting above the mantlepiece. "Where did you get that?" he asked.

Julian looked at where he was pointing. "Hmmm, I dunno," he answered. "Nick bought it."

Callum smirked. "Thought so. You want me to buy you something better?"

I stupidly half-expected Julian to defend my taste in art, but instead he just gushed at Callum. "Thanks! That's so fucking cool of you." He kissed him again.

Callum stuck his empty wine glass out at me. He'd necked it fast; he hadn't taken any time to savour the wine that I'd been saving up for almost two years now. I quickly took his glass, hurried to the kitchen, and filled it again. When I came back out the two of them had stopped talking and were making out, so once again I had to awkwardly clear my throat to get Callum's attention. He just put his hand out expectantly, and I handed him the glass.

As they drank the wine they joked and kissed and groped each other. I watched them both spill red wine probably a dozen times — all over the sofa and the carpet — but they never seemed to notice or care. The whole time they didn't acknowledge me at all, other than to hand me their empty wine glasses for a refill. I could see them start to get more and more drunk, and as they did they got more handsy with each other.

When Callum finished his third glass, he dropped it casually on the ground and leaned into Julian. He kissed him all over his neck, and started unfastening his belt. Julian quickly reciprocated, knocking back the last of his wine, setting the empty glass clumsily on the floor and tugging Callum's tee shirt off. They clumsily, drunkenly, undressed each other while not taking their eyes or their lips off each other for a moment.

Callum had to stand up to get his trousers off, and for the first time I got to see his naked body close up. He was toned and lean, with none of the soft flabbiness that I'd started to accumulate around my hips and gut. I could make out every muscle of his shoulders, arms and back; they weren't giant like a weight-lifter or anything, but they were perfectly defined. When he removed his trousers it revealed a sculpted ass, framed in black briefs of the same style as the ones he'd convinced Julian to start wearing for him.

When he shifted his weight on his foot he was suddenly side-on, and I finally saw what it was about Callum that had turned Julian into the insatiable cockwhore he'd become. Julian had already told me Callum was hung, and I'd seen it a hundred times watching the video Julian had sent me. But I still wasn't prepared for the sight of it in real life, this perfectly packaged bulge in his briefs. It looked like he was smuggling a large banana in there, and it wasn't even hard yet.

Then he slowly pulled his briefs off, and his thick, long cock flopped out. I could see now why Julian hadn't wanted me to fuck him, and probably never would. There was no way I could compete with that. My cock had sprung to attention, but as hard as it was right now, it was still smaller than Callum's cock soft.

Julian greedily took Callum's cock in his mouth and started giving him the sloppiest, messiest blowjob I'd ever seen. He kept gagging on it, but continued taking it deeper. Each time Callum pulled his cock out a trail of Julian's spit would dangle from it; Julian would gasp for breath after being choked with it, but then go straight back for more. The more he sloppily sucked on it, the harder and bigger Callum's cock got, until it was so long and thick I couldn't quite believe he could even fit it in Julian's mouth.

Eventually Callum withdrew his cock, kissed Julian hard, then asked him, "You wanna rim me, babe?"

Julian nodded enthusiastically. He got on his knees on the floor in front of the sofa. Callum sat down on the sofa, resting his legs onJulian's shoulders so his ass was exposed and lifted off the cushion. Julian leaned in, raising Callum's legs higher, until his thighs were vertical and his hole was accessible. Then slowly, gently, he nestled his face in Callum's ass and started to eat out his hole.

Callum moaned in approval. I couldn't see exactly what Julian was doing; all I could see was his head buried in Callum's ass, moving around while Callum writhed in pleasure. "Yeah, babe," he whispered.

Now that Callum was facing me, he seemed to finally remember I was present. For the first time since they'd started undressing he looked right at me, and smiled smugly. "Get closer."

I wasn't sure I heard right. I didn't want to intrude. But then he told me again. "Come over here, get a closer look."

I crept across the room, nervous about breaking Julian's concentration. I got down beside him, only inches away, where I could see what he was doing. He was teasing Callum's hole with his long tongue, tickling it, running it from hole to taint and back again, over and over. Then he dove in, so his mouth was firmly planted on Callum's hole, and I could no longer see what his tongue was doing. Callum's moans got louder, and he was swearing, "Fuck. Holy fuck." There was a small pool of precum on his torso where his erect cock was leaking all over him.

Eventually he must have been getting too aroused to take it any longer. He pushed Julian's face away. He lowered his legs so he was sitting on the sofa again. His huge, thick cock was wet at the tip from where Julian's rim job had made him leak. "Get on." It was an order, but it was the first time that night that I'd heard a hint of pleading in his voice, like he was desperate for Julian's ass.

Julian didn't hesitate for a second. He straddled Callum and lowered himself down onto his waiting cock. Despite the size, his hole swallowed it in one fluid motion, like it was its purpose. Julian let out a whimper as it filled him, and he just sat there, still, for a few seconds. Then he started to slowly ride it, up and down. From where I was only a foot away, I watched in awe and fascination as Callum's bare cock slid in and out of Julian's hole, stretching it to its limits. I marvelled at how he could do that without lube, till it dawned on me that he was probably still lubed up with Callum's semen from their last fuck.

In all my years with Julian I'd never seen him bottom before. But right now he looked like he was born to ride Callum's cock. He looked like he'd found his purpose in life, and everything else had faded away. His eyes were closed, his head tilted back, a blissful expression on his face as he started to ride harder and faster. Callum sucked and bit on his nipple and he cried out. Whether it was pleasure or pain I couldn't tell, because it was a sound unlike any he'd ever made with me.

They carried on like that, lost in their own little universe where the only things that existed were each other. They kissed, passionately, urgently, like they needed each other so desperately they didn't know how to deal with it. I'd watched Julian fuck before, but I'd never seen him make love with another man like he was doing right now.

My dick was in agony. It was so hard it felt like every bit of blood in my body had rushed to my dick and couldn't disperse, and every vein was going to explode. I pulled it out of my pants and started to tug at it furiously. Callum and Julian were both so consumed by each other that they didn't even notice.

I shouldn't have, though. I should have showed some restraint. Because after about two minutes of jerking myself off watching them make love, I shot a wad of cum into my hand. Once that was done I had to sit there, like a fucking loser, watching them continue to fuck intimately and intensely.

When Julian came it was without warning. He just let out a gasp, and unleashed jets of cum that shot up into the air and landed on Callum's chest. He hadn't even touched his own cock the entire time, Callum had made him ejaculate solely from being fucked. Julian's orgasm set Callum off: he pounded Julian's ass and with a howl he came inside him. He finished off with three hard thrusts, getting every last bit of his seed out. Then Julian collapsed on top of him, panting in Callum's arms for a couple of minutes.

In that intimate moment post-orgasm, I felt like an intruder. I knew the appropriate thing to do was to make myself scarce, so I quietly exited the room to find towels to mop up the mess. When I came back into the room, however, I found Callum using one of the cushions from my sofa to wipe Julian's semen off his stomach. I offered him the towel, somewhat redundantly, but he just ignored me.

"Hey, so dancing, then?" Julian asked him.

"For sure. You choose the club."

I must have looked confused, because Julian clarified for me: "We're going to head out again. It's still kinda early. And I'm like, just the right amount of buzzed."

"Oh. I'd assumed—"

"Did you think I was going to stay here drinking cheap whiskey and sleeping in your queen sized bed?" Callum asked. "Fuck off. We're going out, then we're going home to my place." He turned to Julian. "I just gotta go piss and then I'm good to go."

As he walked down the hallway towards our bedroom I called out to him, "Hey the bathroom is the other way." I turned to Julian, wanting to say something about tonight, but not really knowing where to start.

"When do you think you'll be back?"

Julian shrugged. "Dunno. When my ass is too sore to go on fucking." He changed the subject: "Was it hot? Watching him fuck me."

I admitted it was. "He's really had an effect on you."

"Like you wouldn't believe."

"You… you have feelings, don't you? For Callum." It made me nervous to ask, even though I was pretty sure what the answer would be. I guess I just wasn't sure if I was ready to hear it.

Judging by the look on Julian's face he seemed surprised I'd even asked. "Yeah. Totally. You don't have a physical connection with someone the way we do without falling in love."

"In love?" My stomach churned. I hadn't expected to hear that word.

I wanted to ask more, but at that moment Callum returned, and put his arm around Julian. "Ready?"

"Of course." He kissed Callum, then turned to me. "Guess I'll see you sometime?" It was like he was speaking to an acquaintance or something.

I nodded. "Have fun."

They headed for the door, but then Callum stopped as if he'd just remembered something he'd almost left behind. He walked over to the mantle, and took down the painting hanging above it. Before I could challenge him he told me, "I'm just going to put this out with the trash. Maybe someone will want it, you know. And I'll send Julian home with something decent to go in its place."

Then they were gone, off to party till fuck knows when. I was shattered; I felt like I'd just been fucked as hard as Julian was. I decided to go to bed, and maybe play with my dick replaying their sex in my mind as I drifted off to sleep. But first, I got some salt and soda water and tried to clean the red wine stains out of the sofa and the carpet.

In the bedroom I found one last surprise though. As soon as I came into the room the smell hit me. At first I didn't know where it came from, but then I saw the wet sheets. There was one big wet patch, and trails of wet all over the bed. I knew instantly what it was, but I got up close to give it a sniff to be sure. That asshole, he'd pissed all over my bed, more than once judging by the amount of piss soaked through my sheets. For a second I thought about stripping the covers off and remaking the bed. But instead I just lay down, in the cold wet of Callum's piss, and started masturbating again. I inhaled it deeply, thinking about how Callum had made my husband, and now my house, his territory.

CHAPTER 6

For the first three weeks since that night when he'd brought Callum over to our place, Julian hadn't said a word to me. No calls, no texts; I'd messaged him occasionally, but every time he just left me on read. Even though I'd gotten used to waking up alone, I still missed the sound of his voice so much.

As much as I missed him, it still turned me on so damn much to think about what he must be doing with Callum. I'd jerk myself off multiple times every day: first a quick wank in the morning when I'd wake up alone and imagine them waking up together, and again at night when I'd make myself cum from the memory of seeing them make love. I hadn't sat in that spot on my sofa since that night; I'd sit across from it, so I could picture them still there, their two bodies pressed against each other while they fucked. That spot on the sofa was like a shrine to them — the cushion encrusted in Callum's dried semen, and the carpet in front of the sofa still stained with red wine. Although I thought Callum had acted like an asshole that night, thinking about the way he dismissed me and disrespected me made me cum harder each time I sat there reliving it.

I would have believed Julian had forgotten about me entirely if it wasn't for the note and the painting I found when I got home on the Tuesday night three weeks in to his absence. The painting was leaning against the wall, near the spot where Callum had taken down my painting that night. It was big - bigger than the one it was replacing. Although there was no face visible, I recognised it instantly: Julian, face down, sprawled across crumpled sheets. One leg stretched out straight, the other bent ninety degrees. His perfect, firm, round ass the focal point of the portrait. The brush strokes perfectly capturing every shadow of his toned frame. And in the bottom right corner, a signature: Callum Cross.

On the mantle next to it was a small note:

This is to replace the one Callum got rid of. Love u

I sat on my sofa jerking myself off to that painting every night after that. It made me angry and jealous that Callum, as well as being handsome, hung and rich, was also such a talented artist. And that just made it hotter to sit there, imagining the room in which he painted that image — stinking of the sex they'd had, warm and bright in the afternoon sun. Julian lazily dozing, then waking up and beckoning Callum away from his canvas to make love to him again.

Having this painting right there in my living room made me feel more humiliated than ever, but it also allowed me to finally feel a little closer to them.

I'd tried to leave Julian alone after that, and not bother him with my whiny, insecure phone messages. But in the end I'd had to message him about a week later to remind him about Lachlan's birthday brunch; I'd hoped he'd be home before I'd need to nag him, but I should have known he wouldn't be.

By the morning of the brunch I'd resigned myself to the

fact that I'd need to go alone, and I figured I'd just need to make up an excuse for Julian when he didn't show.

There was no sign of Julian when I got to the cafe, but everyone else was there. I greeted everyone and grabbed a seat at the table.

"Hey I'm sorry Julian isn't here," I said to Lachlan.

"It's all good," Lachlan replied, before I'd even had a chance to lie to his face with some made-up excuse for where Julian was. "I caught up with him and Callum a couple of nights ago before they left."

I didn't know Lachlan had even met Callum before. Of course I should have known. "Left?"

"To Greece" he replied. "That's what you meant, right?"

I saw in Lachlan's face the moment the penny dropped. "You didn't know?" He looked awkward and a little panicked for a second as silence descended on the table. I felt my cheeks starting to burn with embarrassment.

It was probably only a second but it felt like an eternity, until Josh broke the silence. "Shit, he didn't know!" He was grinning ear to ear, loving every second of seeing me humiliated. "Dude, your husband's sunning himself on a greek island with his boyfriend right now. And he didn't even tell you he was leaving!"

A couple of the other guys laughed, while a couple of others gave me looks of pity. I could feel my cheeks get hotter and more flushed from the embarrassment of it: my husband was on holiday with another man, and all my friends knew except me.

"They've been in Santorini, Mykanos, Skiathos, all over the place," Josh volunteered. "It looked like they were having fun."

"I know, right?" Lachlan agreed, chuckling. "Those pics from the circuit party looked awesome."

"And those beaches, man, stunning," Davey piped up.

"I'm surprised they've even left their hotel, to be honest," Josh said. "Why get out of bed when you've got Callum fucking you?"

People nodded. Everyone seemed to know all the details of their holiday, while I didn't even know they were out of town. "What pics?" I asked nervously.

"On Julian's socials," Lachlan told me. "You don't even follow him?" He pulled out his phone, brought up Julian's feed, and handed the phone over to me.

Fuck. I knew Julian had a profile but as far as I knew he never even used it, so I'd never bothered to follow him. But as I scrolled through the pics I discovered that he'd become much more active over the last month or two. And I discovered that my cuckolding had become much more public than I'd realised.

There were photos of the two of them relaxing poolside. Dozens of them, from different days, the two of them wearing different bathing suits each day. Julian seemed to have a whole wardrobe of skimpy speedos that hugged his ass and the bulge of his junk. Shots of him sunbathing, drinking cock-tails, pulling himself out of the pool. The two of them kissing, their wet bodies pressed together.

There were photos of the two of them on a yacht, electric blue sea and cloudless sky behind them. Professional-looking photos of Julian, modelling expensive clothes that Callum must have bought for him: shirts unbuttoned most of the way down, tight pants that showed off his ass. The kinds of clothes he never wore around me. There were photos of him and Callum partying with groups of handsome, smiling men — in opulent-looking bars, and what I assumed must be Callum's own home. The two of them at some kind of rave, dressed only in jockstraps and harnesses, arms around each other. Photos of them walking in streets of sun-bleached stone, or hiking in hills overlooking the sea. And domestic scenes too:

Julian and Callum cooking, eating, even lying together in bed, just in case there could be any remaining doubt about the nature of their relationship.

Callum was tagged in some of the pics, so I had a look at his feed too. There was more of the same; but while Julian only had a hundred or so followers, Callum had over sixty-thousand. That meant sixty-thousand people all seeing how my husband had become his boyfriend. It made me feel thoroughly cuckolded, and so horny I could barely stop myself from running to the restroom and knocking one out then and there.

I'd been so consumed by the pics that I'd only half-noticed the conversation — the innuendo, the laughs at my expense as they talked about how envious they were of Julian and Callum and what the two of them must be getting up to. I was flustered and horny and filled with angst, but I did my best to just smile and laugh through the conversation. Eventually they moved on to something else, and I tried to pretend I was paying attention. But the whole time, all I could think of was the two of them and their romantic holiday. It was the longest brunch of my life.

As soon as I was home I was back on their feeds, horny again and analysing every photo to see what facets of their relationship I could glean from the photos. That's when I noticed the call to action in Callum's bio to 'check out my fan site'. My heart almost stopped when I saw that. As I hurriedly thumbed in my credit card details to get myself subscribed to Callum's page, my mind was in an absolute frenzy of dread and anticipation. I knew what I was going to find, but I couldn't quite believe it.

But even my wildest predictions hadn't prepared me for what I found. I was expecting half a dozen videos, but there were over a hundred. Just from the last two months. And as I scrolled through the titles, I quickly discovered they weren't vanilla, either. Some were, of course: there were videos of the two of them making love, intensely, the way they'd done in my house three weeks earlier. And there were others that were just kind of generic porn, like Callum holding the phone, filming his big cock dipping in and out of Julian's ass as he fucked him from behind. But there was some kinky stuff too, which I was not expecting at all. Julian tied up and fucked on the bed, or Julian with his hands bound behind his back. Watersports, outdoor sex, even the two of them fucking at parties in front of their friends. I knew Julian was usually down for a lot of things, but this was a side of him I'd never seen before.

I could have kicked myself for not checking their social media before. All this time that I'd been so desperate to see what they did without me around, and it had been here online the entire time. All I had to do was pay for it. Pay to watch my own husband being fucked by another man who was already so wealthy he didn't need a cent of my money.

The next couple of days were kind of a blur to me. I still went to work, and went through the motions like a zombie. But every other minute of every day I was watching videos of Julian being fucked every way possible, for all Callum's fans to see. I stayed up till all hours of the morning, watching and rewatching every single video till I'd seen them all dozens of times, and I was exhausted, my dick raw from pleasuring myself.

I saw that weekend that they were on their way home. Their last night there, Julian posted a pic on his social media feed of the two of them on the beach at sunset, kissing, their hands clasping each other. The caption read:

Had the most magical time with my amazing bf at one of the
most incredible places I've ever been. Don't want it to end.
Thanks babe for taking me on the trip of a lifetime, love you
so fkn much

Seeing the words "love you" made my heart sink and my dick pulse at the same time. I came after about thirty seconds of jerking off to that post. But as soon as I'd cum, my heart sank even more. I knew now that I'd let things go far too far, and that if I didn't do something now I was going to lose him for good. If I hadn't already.

At least he was coming home now, and we could talk.

But we didn't. Even though he was back in town I still didn't hear from him for another six days. He must have gone straight to Callum's without it even occurring to him that he should come home, or even get in touch.

When he finally came home it was a Tuesday night, and it was a total surprise to me. He greeted me like a friend that he loved dearly, but there wasn't a hint of desire there.

"I've missed you," I told him. "I've missed you so fucking much." The tears started as soon as those words left my mouth.

"I've missed you too," Julian said, but with a whole lot less emotion than me.

I took a deep breath. "Julian, we need to talk."

He nodded. "Yeah, I guess we probably do," he agreed. "Before we get into it though, do you want to eat Callum's loads out of me?"

Of course I did. Julian didn't even need to wait for my answer, he just dropped his pants and bent over the dining table. "There's two loads in there," he told me. "Big ones."

I went to town licking the cum out of Julian's sloppy, sticky hole while he told me about the sex he'd been having. "I was riding him all morning," he told me as I lapped at the salty cum. "He found me sunbathing by the pool and he couldn't resist, he just lay down on the sun lounger and I rode him right there. He didn't even take my trunks off, he just pulled them out of the way and fucked my hole. I came a big load in my fucking speedos from him hitting my ass so deep."

I moaned as my hard dick released its load in my pants. Fuck, it was too soon, too quick. It had only been a few seconds and I wanted it to last for at least a little longer.

Julian must have realised from the little moan I made that I was done, because he hitched up his pants and stood up. I was gutted; I knew there was guaranteed to be a whole lot more cum in him I hadn't gotten to taste yet. He sat down on the sofa — the same spot where I'd watched him get fucked over a month ago now — and gave me a serious look. "Okay babe, I guess we should talk."

I didn't know quite where to start. I'd had everything straight in my head, all the things I wanted to say, but then he'd gone and put his slick, cum-soaked asshole in my face and now all my thoughts were in complete disarray. I desperately tried to get my thoughts in order, but nothing came to me.

"I'll start," Julian offered. "You know I love you, right?"

I nodded, even though I was much less sure of that than I used to be.

"I'll always love you and you'll always be my husband. But Callum and me, we have a really fucking intense connection. He makes me feel ways that you never have."

I nodded again, not daring to look him in the face. "Where does that leave me though?" I asked, staring at the ground as I asked the question.

"Like I said, you're my husband and you'll always be my husband. It makes me happy, knowing you're here waiting for me, and that I can come home and you'll lick the cum from my ass and forgive everything I've done. This is great for both of us: I get the best sex of my life, multiple times every day, and a man who totally owns me. And you get to live out your total cuck fantasy, way more intensely than when I just fucked around with the odd random from the bar."

It was all true, but all wrong at the same time. "I miss you though," I told him, angrily. "I see you like once a month, you never call me or text me back. It's like you've forgotten I exist. I mean yeah, I get off on you cucking me with him, but you've completely disappeared! I don't even know if I'm still being cucked or if you've just left me for good."

"I haven't left you," he reassured me. "But don't ask me to stop spending time with Callum."

I shook my head. "I'd never. That's not what I'm saying. I see how happy you are with him. I've seen how he fucks you. I'd never want to try and make you give that up."

"Then what?"

"I don't know!" I was exasperated, and I was letting my emotion get to me. "I guess... I guess I just don't want to be left out."

"That is literally the point of cuckolding, isn't it?" Julian snapped back, impatiently.

"Not like this though. I need to be involved. You know I had to find out from our friends that you were on holiday with him? And that your relationship was all over social media? For fuck's sake, Julian, I just want to be included, just a little bit. I don't want to have to pay nine ninety-nine a month to get to see you with him."

Julian was silent for a little bit. "Yeah, of course," he conceded. "That's fair enough. I'm sorry, you know. To be honest I just get a little caught up sometimes because Callum makes me forget about everything else, including you. When I do remember to think about you I just tell myself that you're probably enjoying getting cucked, because honestly, that gives me an excuse to stay another night with Callum instead of coming home."

That admission shocked us both into silence. In my head I wrestled with whether to yell at him, or to tell him that if he was that averse to coming home maybe he shouldn't bother anymore. In the end though, my voice shaking, I just told him, "I'm glad you came home. I don't want to lose you."

Julian's expression softened. "You're not gonna lose me," he said, giving me a reassuring smile. "I'm here now. Three whole nights; Callum's away in New York."

"Three nights isn't much," I said sullenly, like a kid who didn't get the toy he wanted.

"Be happy for that. Three hours without his cock is torture, let alone three days. If I didn't have to, if he didn't leave to go out of town for work so often, I don't know if I'd ever leave." He chuckled as he stared wistfully off into space. "I'd just stay in bed, all day every day, just being fucked till he's spent."

I thought of all the loads it would take for Callum to be spent. That reminded me of the load I'd just eaten out of Julian's ass, that I could still taste in my mouth. It made me a little hard again.

"Anyway," Julian said, snapping himself out of his daydream, "When he's back, I got an idea for you that might help you feel a little better about the whole situation."

"Oh yeah?" I asked, intrigued.

"Callum said you could come over to his place for the weekend. You might get to see us in action. Or at least hear us." He laughed to himself at that idea.

"Really? You'd let me come over?"

Julian nodded. "For sure. Callum's housekeeper's got the weekend off so we need someone to clean up after us."

The eager smile dropped off my face instantly. "Wait, so I'd just be there to do housework?"

"I thought you'd like that. I mean if you don't want to—"

"I want to come!" I interrupted him before he could finish his sentence. "Of course I do. It sounds hot, listening to you guys fuck and cleaning up after you." I wasn't lying, either. The thought was already getting me a little hard.

"Cool, that's settled then," Julian replied, looking pleased with himself. "And in the meantime, you got your husband back for three whole nights. So what do you want to do? We can do anything you like. Except sex, of course — that's not for you anymore."

CHAPTER 7

My throat was dry and my heartbeat was drumming in my ears as I stood on Callum's doorstep. I couldn't quite come to terms with the fact that I was about to be invited into his house, and into the life that he'd built with my husband.

The door opened. Callum was wearing a black singlet that hugged his chiseled torso and exposed the smooth skin of his muscular shoulders, and grey sweatpants that hugged the outline of his meaty cock. He didn't even look at me, he just stepped forward and scooped Julian up into his arms and kissed him. Julian sighed contentedly as Callum's strong arms wrapped tight around him.

"Missed you," Callum told him.

"Missed you so much," Julian whispered back.

They stood kissing, arms wrapped around each other, for a minute or so, while I just stood there awkwardly. Eventually they uncoupled, and that's when Callum looked at me for the first time. "Come in, Nick."

I followed Callum through the front door into a spacious, double-height foyer with a large winding staircase in its centre. It seemed a little like a modern museum or something; sun streamed in the tall windows, lighting up the white walls

65

that were peppered with paintings. "I'll show you around," Callum said. It sounded more like an instruction than an offer. He started up the stairs, Julian sticking close beside. He didn't gesture for me to follow — he didn't even really look at me — but the instruction was implicit so I hurried up the stairs behind him.

At the top of the staircase he stopped and pointed right. "Our bedroom's that way. You only come near it if you're told to. Got it?"

My dick jumped just a little, thinking about the bedroom my husband slept in with Callum each night. "Yes. Definitely."

Callum turned and walked in the other direction. Julian sauntered after him and I followed, a few steps behind. Like a servant. "This part of the house is where staff stay." He stopped at one of the doors, and pushed it open to reveal a small room sparsely furnished with a single bed, a chest of drawers and a small TV on the wall. "This is your room for tonight. You might as well put your bag down now."

I did as I was told. Callum didn't wait for me, he was already headed back down the hall the way he'd come, so did one quick scan of the room and then hurried after him and Julian.

"You're filling in for the housekeeper," Callum explained as he walked. "The duties basically involve keeping everything clean and tidy, bringing us what we ask for, and helping out with any jobs that need to be done around the house. In terms of cleaning, that means making sure every room is clean at all times. Things put away, floors vacuumed and mopped, surfaces cleaned. In terms of other stuff: you need to bring us drinks when we ask for them, be available whenever we call, go get us whatever we tell you to. You need to help Johannes in the kitchen: cut and prep, carry food out to us, do dishes. That kind of stuff."

He started descending the staircase. "We're having some

friends around for dinner tonight. So I want you to pay particular attention to all the entertaining areas - the lounges, dining room, outdoor seating area - make sure they're immaculate. Help Johannes get dinner ready. Be on hand to bring out the food and drink while we have people here. Clean up after dinner. Then tomorrow you can bring us coffee in the morning, clean up anything left over from tonight, and do the laundry."

At that point he stopped, turned, and looked at me properly for the first time since I'd entered the house. "Understood?"

"Yes," I answered, looking at the floor because I felt too intimidated to look him in the face.

Callum headed as though he was going to lead me into a tour of the rest of the house, but then instead opened a door, just past the bottom of the staircase. "You can start in here."

It was a guest bathroom, completely white except for the pale grey marble floor tiles and bench tops, and the set of identical, deep brown glass bottles of soaps and hand lotions. I walked in and looked around. The room was spotless. I looked at Callum, confused. "You want me to clean this room?" I asked nervously, afraid I was missing something obvious.

"Yeah. It's about to get real messed up," he replied.

Before I could contemplate what he meant by that, Callum reached into his sweatpants and pulled out his cock. He let go of it and let it flop down, limp but hefty. For a second nothing happened, but then he began to let loose a thick, powerful jet of piss. A second later the smell of it hit me, strong and pungent. Callum swayed his hips and his meaty cock flopped from side to side, the stream of piss flailing around and splashing all over the tiles and the wall.

I was so taken aback I think I just stood there, slack-jawed and silent, while he pissed all over the bathroom floor. He had his usual arrogant half-smirk on his face; I looked over at Julian, and he was trying his best not to laugh.

When he was finally done, Callum shook himself off; his cock looked so solid and weighty in his hand that I was simultaneously turned on and angrily jealous of him. He put his cock back in his pants, and left the room. "Clean it up," he called out after him.

I just stood there for a while, a little shocked, soaking up the stench of his piss. It smelled just like my bedroom that night he'd belittled me in my own home; the smell made my dick come to life. Eventually I shook myself out of it, and decided I'd better go looking for a mop.

As I mopped Callum's piss off the floor, I wondered what I'd got myself in for. Was this what I really wanted? Cleaning up after that asshole while he made me look more and more pathetic in front of my own husband? I don't know what I'd imagined — being included? Being welcomed into their bedroom to watch them fuck? Whatever foolish expectations I'd had, I certainly hadn't expected to be mopping Callum's urine from the floor while the two of them forgot I was even there.

When I was done I decided to look around. I told myself that I wasn't snooping, I was doing what I'd been instructed: checking the house to make sure it was tidy. I had to admit to myself though that I was doing it more out of curiosity than duty.

When I got to the top of the stairs I could already hear Julian's moans. Callum was obviously giving him a vigorous dicking down, because his moans had this mix of both pain and desperation, and I could hear him begging Callum to keep fucking him just like he was doing. My pants were starting to tent listening to them go at it.

I got a little closer to the room, the sounds getting louder as I got closer. I was cautious not to get too close though, in case they heard my movements. I remembered Callum's instructions to stay away from the bedroom unless told to. I stood there for a few minutes and just let the sound of Julians' bliss wash over me, my cock getting harder and harder in my pants.

I don't know how long I stood there. Eventually though, I figured I needed to leave. I didn't want to get caught listening, and I knew if I stayed much longer I'd find it hard to resist the temptation to creep even closer to the bedroom and get my dick out of my pants to the sound of them fucking. Besides, I figured I should actually do the job that I'd been brought here to do. I reluctantly headed downstairs, disappointed I'd miss out on hearing the moment when Callum filled my husband with his load.

———

Vacuuming and mopping took almost two hours because the room was so fucking huge. Prepping food took another hour. I met Johannes, Callum's chef — a tall, muscular, clean-cut, man in a tight-fitting t-shirt and jeans covered by an apron. We made polite conversation as I helped slice vegetables, and he seemed nice enough. But I could tell from the way he avoided asking me certain questions that he knew all about my relationship with Julian and why I was there, and didn't know quite how to talk about it.

Once I was done I wandered out of the kitchen and into the living area, not entirely sure what job I should tackle next. The big glass doors out to the pool were open wide, so I walked out into the sunshine.

I found Julian out by the pool. He was lying naked on a sun lounger, reading a book. His body looked more muscular than last time I'd seen him naked, but his cock looked exactly like I remembered it.

"Hey babe," I said to him.

"Oh hey," he replied, barely looking up.

"How was it?" I asked.

"How was what?" It took him a second to realise what I was asking. "Oh, yeah, fucking amazing. God, my ass is fucking wrecked."

I was hoping Julian would offer to let me lick the cum out of him like he usually did at home. I didn't know how to bring it up — or if I should even ask — though, so I just kind of stood there expectantly for what seemed like a solid minute or so.

"Two ice teas," Callum's voice said from behind me, startling me.

I turned around to find him standing there, naked, his big meaty cock and balls hanging low. Man, he was toned, and beautiful. He was like the kind of guys you only ever saw in porn.

"Yes sir," I said, instantly feeling stupid that I'd added the 'sir'.

As I disappeared into the house I heard him say to Julian, "You know you don't need to make conversation with him, right? If you keep humouring him he'll think he can just talk to you whenever he wants."

When I returned with the ice teas, neither of them even looked up at me. I just set the drinks down and made myself scarce.

———

I didn't see Callum or Julian again until later that evening. All afternoon Callum had me checking paintings to ensure they weren't crooked, then arranging flowers in every room, then vacuuming where I dropped leaves on the ground from my flower arranging. After that Johannes needed my help with the next stage of dinner and setting out hors d'oeurves. I didn't even see the guests arrive, but I could hear from the kitchen that they all seemed to be enjoying themselves.

The next time I saw them was when I brought out cocktails before dinner. Callum and Julian had both put on clothes by this point; both of them were dressed in expensive-looking but casual clothes — loose-fitting linen that that made them look like they belonged on a beach resort or something. Their guests were a handsome gay couple, slightly older, dressed more conservatively but just as expensively. One of them looked familiar, like from TV or something, but I couldn't quite pick where.

No one acknowledged me as I set the drinks out for them; it was as though I was invisible, an appliance rather than a person. I could see that Julian was completely captivated by Callum, barely taking his eyes off him.

About half an hour later I came out with a second round of drinks, just in time to hear one of the guests ask, "So, you live here too, Julian?"

"Not up until now," Julian told the couple. "But…" He looked over uncertainly at Callum, like he wasn't exactly sure whether he was supposed to say what he was about to.

Callum picked up the conversation for him though. "We actually just talked about it today, and decided that Julian's going to move in permanently."

I almost dropped the tray of drinks when I heard that. I mean, I knew as well as anyone that Julian was no longer living with me in any real sense of the word. But it still stung, hearing them say it out loud, and to see the look of glee on Julian's face when Callum revealed the news. Especially when Julian hadn't said a word to me about it, even though I was right here in the house with them.

Their visitors gushed excitedly. "Oh my god, that's awesome. I'm so happy for you two!" one of them said.

"Congratulations," the other one said. To Julian he said, "You know, when we last saw Callum about six months ago he was making the most of the bachelor lifestyle, so you must have had quite the effect on him to make him settle down this quick."

Everyone laughed at that.

"What can I say? He's definitely had quite the effect on me," Callum admitted.

"Well, you must be doing something really right to tame this stallion!"

"I guess it seemed like the obvious thing to do," Julian explained. "And the right time. I'm around here pretty much all the time anyway. I barely ever go home to my own place. And it just felt right."

"Lucky the houseboy's just turned up with more drinks," said the guy closest to me, finally noticing me hovering awkwardly with the drinks tray. "Because this deserves a toast, right?"

I quickly handed out the cocktails. I stood there for a few seconds, watching as they all toasted Julian and Callum's news. The way they were all so pleased — and the way Julian didn't even really react to my presence — killed me and made my dick swell at the same time.

As soon as I could make an exit, I hurried back to the kitchen, trying desperately to think my way to losing my erection. As soon as I could put down my tray in the kitchen I quickly excused myself for a second, and ran to the bathroom. Once I was alone I pulled my hard dick out of my pants, and started to stroke it in a fever. But I knew I couldn't keep going. I didn't have time; I had work to do. And I knew if I could make it through the evening without letting myself cum, it would be so much better later on. So I put it away, washed my hands, and stared at myself in the mirror until I was able to feel my erection subside.

For the remainder of the evening I hung out in the kitchen, listening to Callum and Julian and their guests laugh and joke with each other. Every now and then I'd bring out drinks or food, but each time I did, no one seemed to notice I was there. Not even my husband.

As I cleared up the plates from dinner, though, Callum said to me, "Hey, cuck, get us another bottle of wine, would you?"

I could feel my face go bright red as I hurried out of the room. As soon as I was through the door I stopped — even though I knew I needed to get out there with the wine, I was so embarrassed that I just needed to stop for a minute and let my heartbeat return to normal. I leaned against the door, and took a couple of deep breaths.

From the other side of the door, I heard one of the guests speaking."How come you call the houseboy 'cuck'?" he asked.

I heard Julian laugh at the question. It was Callum who replied though. "Oh, that's Julian's husband. He's a cuckold."

"What? Wait, he's your husband? Your *current* husband?"

"Yeah, we're married" Julian admitted. "I haven't seen much of him lately though."

"Sorry, I don't get it. What's the deal with you guys?"

Callum laid it out for them. "Julian's husband's a cuckold. You know what that is, right? A guy who likes to see his partner get satisfied by another man better than he can do it himself. He brought Julian around here one night, and I guess I satisfied him enough that he kept coming back for more."

There was a whole lot of laughing, before Julian piped up. "He definitely satisfied me. You know, I was a top till I met Callum."

They all laughed again. "Oh yeah, we understand," one of the guests said. "Everyone's heard about Callum's reputation!"

More laughing. When it died down, their other friend asked in a half-whisper,"So that guy in there, he's your actual husband? And you left him for Callum? But he just hangs around serving you drinks?"

"Yeah pretty much." It was Julian's voice. "Well I mean, I haven't left him. We're still married. I just don't see a whole lot of him because I'm with Callum all the time. He's not usually here serving us drinks, either. He's just here for the weekend, while the usual houseboy's away. Thought we'd do something nice for him, you know?"

The whole table laughed again. I felt completely humiliated.

"And he's... he's okay with it?"

"Yeah. Like I think he gets a bit jealous and sad sometimes. But he gets something out of it too, because he gets turned on by knowing Callum's giving me what he can't. That's what being a cuck is all about. We all win, right? Callum and I get to have each other, I get fucked properly, and Nick gets to get off on thinking about the two of us together."

"Wow. So, what happens now? Now that you're moving in with Callum? Does it mean your relationship's going to be over?"

"Not over." Julian replied. "Well, I mean it's over sexually. It's been over sexually ever since I met Callum. And we don't hang out much anymore. But he's still my husband, we still love each other and all that. He just can't measure up to this guy, you know? Callum just kinda stole my heart... and claimed my ass."

I heard them all laugh at that. I wanted to listen longer, but I was conscious that I'd been standing there listening for too long, and they were waiting on their wine. So I grabbed the bottle, took a deep breath, and pushed open the door.

The conversation had moved on to another topic by now. As I approached the table and filled the glasses, Callum kept talking without acknowledging me, as though nothing out of the ordinary was happening. But his friends couldn't take their eyes off me. The expression on their faces as they watched me was a mix of incredulous and amused; they looked like they could barely contain their laughter. That made me go red as beetroot, which I could tell was just making it funnier for them. I turned and almost ran out of the room; as soon as I was through the door, I heard someone mutter something I couldn't quite make out, and the whole table erupted in laughter.

After that every time I came out — to refresh the water, bring out dessert — I could feel their mocking, judging eyes on me. And Julian didn't even acknowledge me, let alone stick up for me in any way.

Once dinner was over they kept drinking and talking for another hour or so. But by this stage they didn't need me any more, because they'd moved from the dinner table to the sofa, and Callum was pouring expensive whiskey from his liquor cabinet. By this time Johannes was done cooking and had retired to his room, so I just busied myself doing dishes and cleaning up the kitchen alone.

Eventually I heard voices in the foyer, and the door closing as Callum and Julian's friends left. I knew that they probably didn't need anything more from me for the evening, and they probably just wanted me to leave them alone. But I couldn't stop myself from going to find them — I told myself that it was just in case there were any more chores that needed to be done, but if I was being honest it was probably because I was holding out for the slim chance they'd invite me into the bedroom to watch them fuck.

I found them on the stairs, headed up to bed.

"Hi," I managed to squeak. "Is there anything you guys need? Before I go to bed?"

"We're fine, thanks babe," Julian replied, not really even looking at me.

I stood there, watching them climb the stairs. I knew I shouldn't say anything, but the words were busting to get out of me. I needed him to acknowledge what he'd said tonight

— what had seemed like nothing to him, but represented the end of the whole world as I knew it.

"You're moving in with him?" The words echoed in the cavernous room and hung in the air all around me.

Julian turned around and looked at me. "Yeah!" His face was beaming, joy and excitement written all over it. "Cool, right? You excited for us?"

He didn't even realise I'd be upset. "For good?"

He nodded. The expression on his face started to shift from excited to, confused, to full of pity, as he realised I wasn't as happy about it as he was.

"So…" It almost hurt to ask the question: "So, you're leaving me?"

"No, not at all!" Julian shook his head emphatically. He took a few steps down the stairs, like he was coming to take me in his arms and comfort me; but then he stopped as though he'd realised that was a weird thing to do. "Nick, I still love you. You're still my husband and I want it to stay that way, as long as you still want to be my husband."

"Of course I do. I just don't understand. I never see you. You're moving in with him, permanently. Without even telling me. How can you do that and say you still want to be with me?"

"I don't know." He sounded irritated, like he was annoyed at himself for not knowing the answer to the question. "This situation is new to me and I don't really know what it all means."

"Tell me what you do know then," I demanded.

"Okay, fine. I know I don't want to fuck you anymore. I know that my physical relationship is with Callum now, because he makes me feel all kinds of ways you never could. I know that you know that you're a cuckold, and this is your place. Knowing your husband's getting taken care of by a real man. Our relationship's going to be different from now on — I mean, it already is, right? Even if Callum stopped being in my life tomorrow, things would never be the same again. We'll need to work it out as we go. But don't expect me to be home. And don't expect me to make time for you when Callum's around. Because I'm his now."

I nodded, accepting everything he'd said. Feeling those words in the pit of my stomach and my groin.

"This is for the best, you know?" His tone softened. "Callum's the most important person in my life now. Callum's cock is the most important thing in my life. I still love you, so much. But you're second-best now. I think you knew that already, and I think if you just accepted that you'd be a whole lot happier with the situation."

Callum took Julian by the hand, kissed him tenderly on the forehead, and without another word led him up the stairs. Callum didn't even bother looking at me, but Julian turned back once more. "Goodnight, Nick," he said, with pity in his eyes and his voice. "Make sure you remember to enjoy this, okay?"

I just stood there as they disappeared, trying to process what Julian had said. I thought back to that night I'd dropped him off outside this house; I'd never thought for a second that it would end up like this. But to be honest, part of me had always expected that this scenario was the inevitable conclusion of my cuckolding kink. All it had taken was finding a man who was good enough for Julian to give up on one-night stands and keep coming back to him for more.

I don't know how long I stood there, staring into space. But eventually I snapped out of it when I started to hear Julian moaning, taking Callum's cock. I slowly climbed the stairs, listening carefully to his cries and trying to imagine each thrust of Callum's cock inside him. By the time I got to the top of the stairs I was so horny I could feel the wetness in my pants from my leaking dick. I ran down the hall to my room, shut the door behind me, pulled out my dick, and started to stroke it to the sound of them fucking.

Of course, I came after about ten minutes, squirting a load of cum all over my chest. And of course, they were nowhere near done. For ages I listened to the sound of them fucking. On and on, Callum pleasured him relentlessly. It was completely, utterly obvious why Julian would choose sex with Callum over me.

Eventually it had gone on so long that even I — the desperate, neglected cuckold who'd pined for so long to be here just to listen to them — was bored of listening. So I switched on the TV and watched the last half of some old movie I didn't even know the name of.

By the end of the movie, the noises had stopped. It was after one in the morning. I figured I should get some sleep myself, so I turned off the light and got into bed. But as I lay there, getting semi-erect all over again thinking about the two of them spent and asleep in each other's arms, I couldn't sleep at all.

I tried to go to sleep, and I tried to fight the temptation. But in the end I couldn't help myself. I threw the covers off, climbed out of bed, and went out into the hallway.

I walked as silently as I could. The hallway down the staff's end of the house was dark and windowless, but I knew that once I found the place where it turned ninety degrees, it was basically just a straight line to the main part of the house. Closer to the centre of the house and the main stairwell, the big windows let in white moonlight that illuminated the floor and helped me get my bearings. From there, narrow windows punctuated the corridor the rest of the way to Callum's bedroom, lighting my way.

As I got closer to his room, every footstep I made sounded like tap-dancing shoes in huge cavern, and my breath — even though I was trying to barely breathe at all — sounded like a roar. This was such a stupid idea; I was sure I was going to wake them up, they'd both be furious at me for not respecting their privacy, and I'd never be allowed back. I told myself I needed to just go back to bed. But I couldn't. I was so close, and I needed to see them sleeping together.

After what seemed like an endless, slow creep, I finally arrived at the bedroom door. To my dismay, it was shut. *That's a sign,* I told myself. *Just go back to bed.* But I'd come too far now. I clutched the handle, my hand shaking. I started to turn it.

If I made a noise now there was no turning back. All I could do was follow through, and be prepared for the consequences.

But the door latch opened silently. I slowly pushed the door open a crack, then stopped. I waited in absolute silence, holding my breath to listen for the sound of them stirring. But all I heard coming from the room were slow, deep breaths.

I pushed the door open slightly. I couldn't see much, but I was confident there was no movement. I pushed it open a little more, until it was open wide enough that the moonlight allowed me to see what was inside.

There they were, peacefully sleeping. Callum lay on his back, one arm around Julian, who lay with his head nestled into Callum's shoulder and his arm stretched across Callum's chest. Callum's chin and mouth rested on Julian's head, as though he'd been tenderly kissing him goodnight on the forehead and had just fallen asleep that way. They fit together perfectly, and even in their sleep they couldn't bring themselves to be apart.

It was just like I'd imagined it. Seeing them in such a perfect, blissful sleep together in each other's arms stung. I felt physically sick looking at them, like I'd been kicked in the balls. It was completely, unquestionably obvious how perfect they were together. And I knew that meant that from now on, sneaking glances of them like this would be as close as I'd ever get to intimacy with my husband again.

With a sudden, overwhelming urgency I pulled the door as far shut as I could as quickly as I could without making a noise. I crept down the stairs as hurriedly as I could while still staying silent. And as soon as I was far enough away for it to be safe, I pulled out my erect penis and started jacking off feverishly, the image of them sleeping still etched into my brain. Within seconds I was ejaculating all over the floor, holding my breath as I did to stop from crying out.

Once I'd cum I let myself breathe again, trying to keep silent as my chest heaved. Feeling suddenly ridiculous, I realised I needed to clean up the mess I'd made. So I quickly pulled off my t-shirt and used it to mop the semen up off the floor.

I headed back to my bedroom. By the time I got there my eyes were welling up with tears at the realisation that I had well and truly lost my husband to a man who made him far happier. I crawled into the bed, and finally let myself make a sound as I sobbed myself to sleep.

CHAPTER 8

My alarm went off early the next morning. I felt exhausted but I pulled myself out of bed immediately because I didn't want to be late for the first task Callum had given me.

It was silent downstairs. I went to the kitchen and turned on the coffee machine. While it was heating up I looked up a video on my phone to remind myself how to make espresso coffee; it had been years since the last time I'd had to do it, and I while I remembered the basics I couldn't remember how to make a good one.

I made a coffee for myself first, both to wake me up and to check I'd done it right. Once I was satisfied with my technique, I made coffees for Julian and Callum. Then I found a tray and carried the coffees upstairs.

Their bedroom door was still slightly ajar from where I'd left it last night. I pushed it open a tiny bit, not sure if I was supposed to just barge in or not.

The two of them were still asleep. By now they'd changed positions though; Callum was spooning Julian, his arm wrapped around him and his head nestled into the back of his neck.

I cleared my throat, quietly — almost inaudibly. Callum's

eyes flickered though, and opened. I could see that he saw me, but he didn't acknowledge me. I just stood there, holding my tray of coffees.

Callum's body shifted in the bed a little. Julian responded by letting out a tiny moan. Then another, as Callum's body shifted again. Callum's movements began to become more rhythmic, and I realised what he was doing to make Julian respond like that. Half asleep, Julian started to moan in time with Callum's thrusts as he slowly fucked him awake.

I took a step back, to where I could still see enough but hopefully could remain unobtrusive in the shadows. I saw Julian's eyes open as he woke, finally conscious of what was happening to him. "Fuck," he gasped. Callum kissed his neck as he started to fuck him harder.

They continued like that for a few minutes, Julian gasping and whimpering as he took Callum deep inside him. Eventually Callum stopped though. "Break for coffee?" he asked.

"I guess," Julian sighed, disappointed.

"Coffee!" Callum demanded. I was immediately shaken out of my trance, and entered the room.

"Oh hey, babe," Julian said sleepily when he saw me. "Cool, you made coffee already. Nice one."

I went to hand Julian his coffee. "Wait," Callum stopped me. "It looks like a nice morning. Want to go have our coffee outside?" The question was directed at Julian, not me.

The two of them got out of bed. Callum's cock was still erect, but softening, though still thick and meaty. It was still slick from fucking Julian, who was also still hard.

Callum opened the doors out onto balcony. I followed them out, and sat the tray down on the table outside.

The two of them took their coffees from the tray. Julian wandered over to the rail and leaned on it, looking out over the pool, grounds, and the nature reserve that Callum's property bordered onto. Callum came up behind him, placing a hand gently on his lower back, as they both stood there watching the sunrise slowly transforming into a bright, crisp morning.

I just stood there, awkwardly, in the doorway, until Callum finally turned around and noticed me there. "Dude, how 'bout you give us some privacy," he said. Then he turned back, not even bothering to check if I was following his instructions.

I went back into the bedroom, and as I looked back I saw them kissing each other, naked in the golden morning light.

Not sure what to do next, I just loitered in the hallway for a bit. But after ten minutes or so I started to hear the sound of them fucking again, and I realised I wouldn't be needed for a while. I busied myself cleaning, then brought them sparkling water after about an hour. After they'd hydrated, Callum told me, "We're going out for brunch. Good news for you is that you get to wash the sheets." He gave me his usual cocky smirk. "Now get out while we get dressed."

I didn't see them again before they were gone. But as soon as I heard the car leave, I raced upstairs to the master bedroom. The room stunk of sex and sweat, and the white sheets were crumpled, unkempt, on the bed. I got onto the bed, and studied the sheets closely, looking for every cum stain I could find. Every hardened, yellowed spot on the crisp sheets was a sign of something Callum gave Julian that I couldn't.

I pulled the sheets off the bed and gathered them up in my arms. Carrying the bundle down the hallway I buried my face in it and deeply inhaled the smell of sex, the smell of their passion for each other. It made my head swim.

Once I'd put the sweaty, cum-soaked sheets in the wash, I returned to the bedroom. I took my time making the bed with fresh sheets, meticulously straightening them to make a perfect, flawless altar for their sex. I knew they wouldn't notice, and that the sheets would be a mess in a few hours anyway. But it felt good to be able to put that kind of care into preparing their bed and making it the best it could be.

After that I potted. Ostensibly dusting, I mainly used it as an excuse to explore the sprawling house some more. By now it was basically spotless so there wasn't actually much to do.

About lunchtime my phone buzzed. It was Julian. Seeing his name come up on my phone seemed strange and unexpected, which made me realise how long it had been since he'd bothered to call me. I answered it with butterflies in my stomach. "Hey!"

"Hey babe," he replied. "How's it all going over there? Did you enjoy doing the laundry?" He laughed at his own question, and before I could answer he kept talking. "Hey I had a thought. I've already got most of my stuff from our place, like bits and pieces over time. But there are a few things I haven't brought over, so I was thinking maybe you could go pack up the last of my things and bring them back to Callum's place?"

"You want me to pack your things for you? So you aren't even going to come home to do it?"

"That's the idea," he replied, either not noticing the disappointment or just pretending not to. "I'll text you a list of the important stuff. And then whatever else you think I'd want to have with me."

I heard muffled talking on the other end of the line. Then, "Hey, Callum says you can keep that painting though. Something to remind you of me."

Something to remind me of the two of them together.

"Hey we're going to go to this art gallery and then there's a party. So we won't be back till late. So if you just drop the stuff off, the housekeeper should be back any time from about five. And I'll give you a call some time soon so we can catch up. Okay? Bye."

Before I could get a single word in, he'd hung up.

I wondered if I should clean more. But by this stage the

house was so spotless there was literally nothing left to clean. And it was pointless anyway: I wasn't going to see them again.

I quickly did one more quick circuit of the house to make sure there was no more mess to take care of. The circuit led me to the bedroom once more, and now, knowing that I had to leave and may never be back here, I couldn't help myself. I whipped my dick out, sat on the floor and jerked off, staring at the bed and imagining the two of them there, falling asleep in each other's arms after one of their passionate rounds of sex. It felt wrong to be doing that in here, uninvited. But that just made it feel even more necessary; I deserved this, this treat, for all that I'd suffered through and accepted and done to facilitate their relationship.

As usual, it didn't take me long to blow my load. I shot a wad of cum into my waiting hand, did up my pants, and headed to the bathroom to wash the cum off. Once I was clean I slowly, reluctantly headed for the door.

Once outside I paused. I didn't want to close the door behind me; I knew it would lock, then there would be no possibility of changing my mind and going back inside. And who knows how long before I'd be allowed back inside, if ever.

But I did it. With a deep breath I closed the door behind me. Then I got in my car, and headed home to pack up the last of my husband's things.

CHAPTER 9

I looked myself in the eyes in the rear view mirror. "It's not too late to bail," I told myself out loud. I knew that if I wanted to I could turn the car around, drive back down that driveway, and forget that I'd ever thought up this disaster of a plan. Maybe they'd never even know, if they didn't already.

But I also knew already that bailing wasn't realistically an option. It had become apparent in the weeks since I'd last seen Julian, that I'd do pretty much anything — no matter how fucking stupid or pathetic — to be back in his life.

It had been more than two months. Ten weeks and two days, to be exact, since I'd seen my husband in person. Sure, I'd kept up with his life since then. I'd watched his and Callum's social media feeds daily. I'd dutifully paid my subscription to see the photos and videos of them fucking. It turned me on beyond belief to see them together, their physical connection that had bloomed into a tight emotional bond.

Every now and then I'd get some small sign that Julian was still thinking about me. On my birthday, they posted a video of them together in bed. Just before they started to fuck, Julian looked at the camera and said, "This one's going out to my cuck husband for his birthday. Hope you like it, baby." He'd messaged me out of the blue every now and then — actually, it couldn't have been more than twice, come to think of it — with a casual *Hey what's up?* I'd reply, we'd exchange a few messages, then the conversation would die with him leaving me on read.

It wasn't enough. I knew that he and I had to find a new equilibrium for our relationship, one where I didn't expect to be treated like a real husband. But I needed to be near him and for him to remember I existed. And I didn't know how else to do it except through this ridiculous idea, which is why I knew I had to go through with it.

So I took a deep breath and got out of the car. As I walked up to the front door it opened. I expected to be face to face with Julian, or Callum, or both. But instead it was some guy I'd never met before. A skinny twink, well-groomed and smartly dressed.

"You must be Nick," he greeted me, extending his hand. "I'm Flynn."

I took his hand and shook it, managing to get out a mumbled "Hi," as I tried to figure out who he was and why he was the one greeting me.

"Nice to meet you, Nick. Come on in. Mr Cross is tied up with something at the moment but I can show you in." He gestured and I stepped inside.

Being back in that house again was like finding myself in a place I thought only existed in my mind. I'd only ever been there the once, but ever since that night I'd constructed elaborate fantasies in my head of Julian and Callum together in this place, so much so that the house felt like I'd constructed it completely out of my own imagination.

Flynn closed the door behind me, and started walking through to the living area. I followed. "I'm Mr Cross's personal assistant," he explained as he walked. "I'd usually be doing the interviews, but he said he wanted to do yours himself. I understand you're a friend of his partner's?"

"No," I protested, baulking at the accusation. "I'm Julian's... I'm..." I didn't know where to go with that. "Long story, but yeah, pretty much."

Flynn led me over to an area with a couple of sofas and armchairs, and gestured to me to sit down. "If you want to wait here, Mr Cross will be with you in a few minutes." With that he sashayed out of the room, leaving me alone with my nerves.

I could feel the sweat seeping into the armpits of my shirt and dampening my hairline as I waited. Now that it was too late to leave, and now that I knew I was going to be interviewed by Callum himself, I realised that I'd done something incredibly stupid by applying for this job.

I'd seen Callum post on social media about needing to find a new housekeeper. I'd done a whole lot of investigating — maybe more like stalking? — to find out what agency he used to get domestic staff, and I'd cold-called them to express my interest in the job. It had taken some convincing; they'd been sceptical that someone would want to give up a highly paid marketing job to become a housekeeper. But I'd spun them a convincing story, and my experience owning the bar had helped get me across the line.

I knew deep down though, that there was no way Callum was going to give me this job and let him be in his house full-time, creeping onto him and Julian all the time like a pathetic third wheel. So ultimately this interview was just going to be another exercise in humiliation.

At least it would give me something more to jerk off to once I was home.

I heard the footsteps coming down the stairs. A few seconds later Callum walked into the room. Tall, broad-shoul-dered with a confident swagger, he had the beginnings of a smile that looked like he was already mildly entertained by this whole situation. His shirt was unbuttoned about half-way down, showing off the chiseled chest I was so familiar with from the photos and videos I'd seen online. I stood up to greet him, not sure if I should try and shake his hand or not. Not sure if I should even look at him, or just avert my eyes.

Behind him, Julian strolled in. Barefoot, shirtless, he was wearing the tiniest shorts I'd ever seen, made of mesh that was opaque enough that I could make out the silhouette of his black jockstrap underneath. His body had changed since I'd last seen him in person; he was more toned, more muscular, more tanned.

When he saw me he looked confused for an instant, then excited. "Nick!" He lit up, like he was genuinely happy to see me. Seeing him react like that made me almost start to cry tears of joy, but I kept my composure, even as he bounded up to me and gave me a hug. "What the hell are you doing here? It's been months!"

When I didn't answer he turned to Callum. "I thought you said we were interviewing for a housekeeper. What's going on?"

Callum looked at me with that same amused expression as he explained, "Nick's applied for the job. So I thought we should give him an interview."

Julian looked back at me, obviously surprised and maybe kind of puzzled. "You want to be our housekeeper?" he asked. "But what about your job? And the bar?"

"I see we're not wasting any time getting into the inter-view questions then," Callum said. He gestured to the seats and we all sat down, Julian and Callum together on the sofa, hand-in-hand, and me sitting in the armchair opposite them. When we were seated Callum prompted me again: "So, what are you planning to do about your job and your bar if we let you be our house-bitch?"

"I'd leave my job," I assured Julian, "I think the bar will be fine too. I've been helping out there more lately, ever since you've stopped working, but I think that with that guy you hired to pick up your managerial duties, plus paying for an extra couple of bartender shifts, that should cover the work. It'll eat into the profits, but the bar will still break even. And I won't need the money if I'm here all the time anyway."

"But how are you gonna pay the mortgage?" Julian asked. "And what will you do with the house if you're staying here?"

"I'm going to rent it out. I've already put an add up and got the place ready. There's lots of interest. I'll be able to cover the mortgage, for sure."

Julian nodded slowly, processing the information.

"And since I'll be here," I added, "In the servants' quarters, with the bar covered and the mortgage on the house covered, it means I can work full time. Like, twenty-four seven. I can be available whenever you need. And you don't even need to pay me, I can do it for free."

Callum looked kind of annoyed at that. "Dude, you know what I do for a living. You've seen my house. Do you think I need to save a few dollars by getting a houseboy that will work for free? Did you think coming here with a cost-saving proposal was going to get you the job?"

I felt like an idiot. "No," I said meekly, barely even looking at him.

He sighed, like he was disappointed. "Fucking sell yourself man, come on. Tell me why we should hire you."

"Okay." I took a deep breath while I gathered my thoughts, then when I was ready I tried to rattle off all the reasons I'd practiced in front of the mirror at home: "I've worked in hospitality before; I've waited tables, managed front-of-house, managed the bar — with Julian, of course — so I know what I'm doing when it comes to serving guests when you're entertaining people. You've seen me do it before, and you know I've done a decent job."

They gave me no reaction, so I continued. "I know how Julian likes things done around the house, what brands of groceries he likes, all that kind of stuff. So I've got a head start. And I'll work hard to learn the same for you, Callum. I'm happy for you to set any hours you want, I'm happy to have virtually no time off, and I'm happy for you to change my hours without notice. I'd basically be your slave.

"I know I'm not as hot as the houseboys you'd usually have. But the added bonus for you is that you get to humiliate me, whenever you want, in front of whoever you want. In front of my husband. It seems like you enjoy it, and I'm happy for you to do it. More than happy — I'm fucking desperate for you to do it."

Callum chuckled. "I do kinda like that," he admitted. "You're right though, about your body. When I'm entertaining I like to have staff who are a little easier on the eye. Having you wandering around the house wouldn't be great for my personal brand, you know?"

"Maybe he could have some sessions with Gideon, when he's not working?" Julian suggested to Callum. He turned to me and asked me, "Would you be willing to take up a workout regime? Like, a really intensive one, with our personal trainer?"

"Definitely," I promised, without hesitation. It was heartening to see Julian in my corner, arguing for me. "Plus, Callum, you know with me there's no chance Julian's going to cheat on you with me."

That made them both laugh. "That's stating the obvious," Callum agreed.

In the silence that followed I could tell Callum was mulling it over. This was fucking crazy; I'd started out expecting him to laugh in my face, but he was actually considering it. I actually had a chance — even if it was just a small one — that this could happen.

"Tell me why you want this, then," he said finally. "You know Julian's not gonna fuck you. You know you're not getting your husband back. So why do you want to be here in this house watching him and never having him again?"

"I love Julian, with all my heart," I told him. "I know I'm never going to be with him, physically, again. But I want to be in his life."

I looked over at Julian. He gave me a tiny, supportive, reassuring smile.

I continued. "I'm a cuckold. I've always been a cuckold. I've always known that even though I was lucky enough to have Julian fuck me for as many years as I did, ultimately my place was to be replaced sexually by other men who could give him something better than I could. So seeing him become your... your fucktoy, it made sense. It felt natural.

"But losing him entirely, having him disappear from our house and our whole life, that's a whole other level. The last few months have been the hardest thing I've ever had to deal with, him being gone. So I just want to be around, being his cuck, seeing him happy."

"Babe, that's beautiful," Julian said to me.

Callum was silent, still mulling it over. I was acutely aware that my display of emotion just then might have shown him exactly why he wouldn't want me around. So I followed up with more. "So I understand, one hundred percent, that me and Julian are over sexually and romantically; I'm not going to try anything at all."

"I'm not worried about that," Callum replied, dismissively. "I know it wouldn't get you anywhere if you tried." He looked over at Julian. "What do you think? Do you want the cuck around?"

"I think I could maybe go for it, yeah," Julian replied casually.

"You don't sound convinced."

"I think maybe Nick and I should talk for a minute, just the two of us, before we decide anything," Julian decided. "Callum, do you think you could give us a minute?"

"Sure thing." Callum got up off the sofa, unfazed by Julian's request. "Gimme a yell when you're done." Julian didn't let go of Callum's hand until the last possible moment, as Callum walked away.

With Callum out of the room, the two of us — me and my husband — just looked at each other for a second. I was so fucking nervous, and excited, at the prospect that he might actually say yes. But at the same time I was terrified of screwing it up.

Julian broke the silence, eventually. "This isn't some kind of plan to win me back?" he asked.

"No. Not at all," I promised. I meant it.

"You can honestly tell me that you're not harbouring a bunch of feelings for me? Some kind of hope that you being around here is going to rekindle something, and I'm going to come back to you?"

"Well, I mean of course I have feelings for you. You're my husband, and I love you. I love you so fucking much. But I'm not coming here with some fantasy of us going back to how we were. He makes you happy. He makes you sexually fulfilled. I just want to be around to see it."

"You know this wouldn't be polyamory, right? You wouldn't be an equal partner. You wouldn't be a partner at all. You wouldn't have a right to my time. You'd just be the help."

"I understand."

"Could you handle that? Seeing him and I happy, building a life together? Seeing us go off to our bedroom to fuck, knowing we're doing it without giving you a second thought? Being ignored?"

"Yes." I could tell by the way my dick twitched that he was describing exactly what I wanted.

"And you understand this is permanent, right? I mean, you can quit any time, obviously. But my relationship with Callum, I'm in it for the long haul. I'm not going to get a few months in and decide I've had my fun and we can just go back to being a married couple."

I nodded. I'd given up on that prospect months ago.

"I want to stay married to you," he continued. "Maybe not forever; Callum doesn't seem that into the idea of marriage so far, but if he was keen I think I'd probably go for it."

That hurt like hell.

"Im telling you that because I want to be real clear, if you live with us I don't have responsibilities to you, as your husband."

"I know."

"I do love you though. God, it's so hard to explain. I don't even really understand it. You know I've really missed you, right? I mean, I didn't intend to leave you and never talk to you again. It just kinda happened that way because I spent all my time in this kind of fuck-lust with Callum and I forget to get in touch to say hi every now and then. But I still want you in my life. It makes me happy thinking of you being around, even if I'm just ignoring you the whole time.

He paused, while he turned it over in his mind one more time. "So yeah, I think I'd be keen for you to be our new housekeeper," he agreed.

My head swam. "You mean it? You actually mean it?"

He nodded slowly, like he was checking with himself and confirming it in his own mind. "Yeah, sure. This actually seems like a perfect arrangement. We see each other around, we get to stay in each other's lives, and I still get the life I want with Callum. And you expect nothing, other than all your cuckold angst seeing the two of us in love."

He gave me a stern look. "Remember though that I'm going to ignore you. Completely."

I could feel tears welling up in my eyes. "Thank you," I whispered to Julian. "I've missed you so much."

"Before I get Callum back in here though, I want to give you one last chance if there's anything else you need to say to me. Like, as a husband. Before you're just our servant. Because this is probably the last time we're going to talk to each other, as husbands, in a long time."

I thought hard for a second. Of course there were hundreds of things I wanted to say to him, things that had been swirling around in my head ever since he left me sleeping alone that first night he met Callum. But there wasn't enough time to say all of it.

So I went with the one most burning question I had. "Why was it so easy for you?" I asked, fighting back the tears that were starting to well up in my eyes. "Why were you so willing to give up everything we had, so quick, without a second thought?"

Julian's expression hardened; he even looked a little annoyed. "Isn't it obvious? You've seen him, you've seen us together. How could I not fall for him?" His voice softened a little as he explained: "You know, I never expected this to happen when I met him. I thought the two of us would go on being happily married till we're old, with me fucking random guys on the side and not forming attachments. But then I met Callum, and, well, there was no question. He's twice the man you are. There's no way I couldn't fall for him, no way I'd let the chance to be with him pass me by. You're lucky you're a cuck so you can hang around to enjoy it."

I couldn't hold back the tears for another second. As they started streaming down my face I thought about the future with Julian I'd lost. I was so angry, so grief-stricken, for the life we were never going to have together. And I was angry and confused about why the thought of this new life — this life where Julian falls in love with another man and I just watch their love grow while I do their chores — excited me so much that I couldn't wait for it to start.

Surprisingly, Julian came closer, and put his arm around me. I grabbed on to him and sobbed into his shoulder as he held me. I could smell his familiar smell, and feel the warmth of his body against me again for the first time in months. "Thank you," I mumbled as the tears rolled down my face and onto his tanned shoulder.

"Don't get any ideas," he said. "And don't expect me to hug you every time you cry. I'm Callum's now, and you're our slave. But I get that this is a hard moment to deal with."

As I gained my composure a little, Julian pulled away. He held me firmly by the shoulders, and looked me in the eyes. "Last time I'm gonna ask. Are you sure about this? You can handle being our slave, and not my husband?"

I looked him in the eyes as long as I could. "Yes," I replied, as firmly as I could manage. I held his gaze for half a second longer before it was too much; instead I looked down at the hand firmly clasping my shoulder. I just stared at it for a few seconds: the golden skin, the tiny golden hairs, the slightly paler outline where his wedding ring used to be.

"You don't wear your wedding ring anymore," I said through the tears.

"I don't have it anymore," he replied, gently withdrawing his hand from my grasp.

"What did you do with it?"

"Oh, I had it melted down," he replied, offhandedly, as though he'd just assumed I would have expected that to be the case. "Along with some of my other gold jewellery. To make something for Callum."

As if summoned by the sound of his name, Callum entered the room just at that moment. "Cuck's had enough time to decide," he declared. "What's the verdict?"

Julian turned to him and told him cheerfully, "It's on. I want him to do it."

Callum looked me up and down; I must have been a pathetic sight, sobbing the way I was. He extended his hand. "Congratulations then. Sounds like you've got the job. Hope you're not gonna cry like a little bitch when you're on the clock though."

I took his hand and shook it. The whole thing was so surreal I didn't really know how to act. And despite having having just gotten my husband back in my life and having my cuckold fantasy come true, I couldn't help but focus on what Julian had just said.

"What did Julian make for you?" I asked.

Callum looked at me blankly, unsure what I was talking about.

"He's asking about what I did with my wedding ring," Julian clarified.

The penny dropped, and Callum laughed. "Holy shit, he doesn't even know about that yet?"

Julian's face wore a look that was a little guilty, but a little amused. Like a kid who's been caught misbehaving but thinks his antics were hilarious. He didn't say a thing though.

"It's funnier if you tell him," Callum told Julian.

"Okay," Julian caved. "I had my ring melted down. And that chain you bought me for my birthday that I used to wear all the time. And those cufflinks you got me. And some other gold stuff I had. And then I added to it with more gold that I bought with some of the money I get from our online subscriptions. And I had it made into a cock ring."

He made his wedding ring into a cock ring for Callum.

I let that sink in for a bit. I honestly didn't know how he could do it; my wedding ring was the most precious object I owned, and Julian had literally had his one destroyed, just to make something for Callum to wear around his cock when he fucked him.

"Why?"

Julian shrugged. "I figured it would make an impression. I guess he gives me so much — not just his cock, but this whole life with him. I wanted him to know I'm not just taking, I'm prepared to give too. To commit. With some of my most valuable possessions. You know, to show him he's important."

"It worked, too," Callum admitted. "I love it. I wear it all the time."

Julian literally beamed as he smiled at Callum. "Really? You really love it? Fuck, that makes me really happy." He leaned in and gave Callum a little kiss on the cheek.

"Do you think we should let the cuck see it?" Callum suggested.

Julian shrugged again. "Only if you want to. It's yours. It's special. I don't want you to have to share it with him if you don't want to."

"I think it's only fair, considering it's made out of his wedding ring," Callum replied, grinning. "Is this the luckiest day of your life, or what?" he asked me. "Wait right here."

Julian and I stood silently, in an excruciatingly awkward moment that seemed to last an eternity. I had no idea what to say to him.

A minute or so later Callum was back. In his hands he held the thick, weighty gold ring. He held it out on the palm of his hand. "You like it?" He asked. "It took a *lot* of gold to make one big enough to fit around my junk."

I reached out to touch it, but Callum snapped his hand away. "You don't get to touch this," he said, seeming offended that I'd even try.

At that, Callum dropped his shorts, revealing his solid cock. He slipped the ring over his cock and tucked his balls through, then let his heavy package flop back down. He turned to Julian. "You gonna help get me hard, baby?"

Julian didn't need any convincing. He got down on his knees

straight away. He got his face under Callum's cock and slowly, carefully licked his heavy ball sack. Callum let out a contented sigh. "Yeah, that's it baby." With every swirl of Julian's tongue, his cock thickened just a little bit more, and started to slowly rise.

Julian ran the tip of his tongue up the length of Callum's shaft, letting it linger around his frenulum and his piss-slit. As he did, Callum's cock started to pulse, thickening and hardening by the second. Julian knew what he was doing; he must have done this a thousand times by now.

He took the head of Callum's cock in his mouth, and just let it sit there, hardening further. And then, even though by now Callum's cock was so thick and long that it looked like it couldn't even fit, Julian started to take the length of his shaft into his mouth. Callum groaned in absolute delight, and started to slowly pump Julian's face. As he did he looked over at me and gave me a wink.

Finally he withdrew his cock. It was even bigger than what I remembered, swollen, veiny and slick with spit, trails of viscous saliva following it from Julian's mouth. Julian was heaving for breath after having his whole throat filled with Callum's cock, but he didn't wait to recover. He got up onto his feet, and slipped his tiny shorts off to reveal the black jockstrap underneath, the pouch of which was barely containing his own erection. He put his arms around Callum's neck, and they kissed with a level of intensity and familiarity that was beautiful.

Callum took Julian by the ass and lifted him up off the floor. Julian wrapped his arms and legs tightly around Callum, and Callum moved one arm to cradle his lower back while he used his free hand to manoeuvre his cock into place. Julian, held in the air and wrapped around Callum's body, moaned hard as he lowered himself down onto Callum's swollen cock.

"Oh god," he whimpered, as Callum used his hips to

slowly slide his cock in and out of Julian's ass. "Oh god, that's so fucking good."

"Yeah," Callum smiled. "That's my boy. You want my cock, huh?"

"God, I fucking…" Julian couldn't even string a sentence together at this point. "Oh fuck, I fucking, I live… Fuck! I live for it…"

Callum slowly bounced Julian up and down. With each movement I saw his slick cock sliding out, then in again, making Julian cry out each time it pushed in right to the base of his thick shaft. I was amazed by Callum's strength; I wasn't sure I'd even be able to lift Julian off the ground, let alone hold him off the ground and bounce him up and down like a fleshlight on his cock like Callum was. Occasionally Callum would pull right out, all the way to the tip, and I'd be reminded just how huge his cock was. Then he'd plunge it back in, deep, and Julian would wail with pain and delight, and I'd be able to visualise just how far inside that cock was reaching. It was as though Julian was a puppet, being operated by Callum's cock filling his whole core.

And the whole time, I could see the glistening gold of Callum's cock ring, tight around his balls and the base of his cock. Knowing my wedding ring was in there, just one small part of a solid, weighty piece of metal, was such a mindfuck. Knowing that Julian had been so willing to destroy the ring that represented our marriage, just to adorn his new lover's cock, just hammered home what a pathetic cuckold I'd become. And it made my cuck dick spasm like it was trying to escape from my pants of its own accord. I resisted the urge to grab it, knowing that I'd explode in a second if I gave in to the temptation.

They had been so lost in each other that they seemed to have forgotten me. But eventually, Callum's eye caught mine, and he must have remembered I was there watching. He gave me a grin. "Show's over. Get the fuck out and give us some peace. Flynn will call you to organise things with you."

I just stood there, entranced, until he barked at me again. "I said get the fuck out!"

I meekly complied. As I walked out of the room Julian's moans became more intense, more insistent. "Fuck! Fuck! Fuck, I love you so much! God, I love your cock. Yeah, fuck!" The only thing that gave me the strength to walk out the door and miss this moment was the knowledge that I'd be back. There were going to be so many more moments like this, and I'd get to see — or at least hear — so many of them. For the first time it felt like my life wasn't falling apart, it was just beginning.

CHAPTER 10

Letting myself in the security gate and then the front door was kind of surreal. For the first time I had access to enter Callum and Julian's private space of my own accord. I debated whether to ring the doorbell anyway, but thought better of it. I knew they had no staff on site today, which meant either no one would answer, or Callum and Julian would need to stop whatever they were doing and come to the door. The last thing I wanted to do was disturb them.

Wandering up the stairs in silence, I felt like a ghost: an unseen presence stalking through the house, lingering from a past life to watch the new inhabitants of my marriage. I wondered — yet again — whether I'd made a terrible mistake doing this. But even if I had it was too late now, I'd already quit my job, put my stuff in storage, and signed the contract for tenants to move into my house this weekend.

When I reached the top of the stairs I could faintly hear the sound of them fucking. I put down my bags and crept carefully, silently down the hallway towards their room. For a few minutes I stood, listening to the slow, rhythmic rocking of the bed and Julian's whispered moans. My dick got hard instantly, and I longed to touch it. But I brushed that aside in my mind; I knew I'd need to show some restraint, because if I gave myself permission to get my dick out every time their antics turned me on I'd never get anything done around the house.

After I'd let myself listen for what felt like long enough, I pulled myself away. I took my bags to my room and started getting my room set up. It was small and pretty sparse, and as I took my clothes from my bag and neatly put them in my new chest of drawers I felt like a monk, unpacking his meagre possessions into his cell in a monastery, readying for a life of austerity. I guess there were a lot of parallels between my life and a monk's, because from today I was going to be living a life of chastity, obedience and service to my new masters.

As I unpacked, their fucking started to get loud enough that I could hear them from my room. I tried to pay enough attention to enjoy the sounds, while simultaneously focusing on the task at hand. I was going to have to get good at that.

I took out the few nicknacks I'd brought with me: my favourite planter, for which I'd need to find myself a plant to brighten up the room; a calcite geode and a few of my favourite books which I set on my dresser; and a photo of Julian and I together, which I slid into the frame of my mirror to hold it in place. As I secured the photo I studied it. The two of us were smiling; we were happy, and close. It seemed like forever ago. Now on a daily basis I saw the same kind of photos on my social media feed, but with my face replaced by the face of the man that had ousted me from my role.

After a while the fucking reached a crescendo, and then stopped. By now I was finished unpacking the few belongings I'd brought with me. I wondered whether I should go get them a couple of glasses of water, or whether to leave them alone, but I couldn't make up my mind.

A minute or so later I was startled by a noise behind me. I

jumped, and turned around, to find Callum standing in my doorway. He was naked, his ripped body glistening with the sheen of an energetic fuck-session. I couldn't help but be drawn to his cock. It was flaccid but still huge, slick with a layer of lube and semen from fucking my husband.

"Up here," he ordered, seeing me ogle his penis. I flushed red, embarrassed to be caught staring, and looked at his face. At least for a second; I always felt the need to avert my gaze.

"So you're unpacked then." An observation, not a question.

I nodded.

Callum looked around the room, and his brow furrowed into a scowl when he saw the photo on my mirror. He walked over to it, pulled it out from the mirror-frame, and dropped it on the floor. "What the hell, man?" he asked angrily. "Don't go putting up photos of my boyfriend in your bedroom. That's just fucking weird."

I couldn't look him in the eyes, so instead I just looked at the photo on the floor. "Sorry," I told him. "I didn't think."

"Okay. You're still learning the rules so I'll cut you some slack." He changed the subject. "Now you're here we decided on a new rule: we want clean sheets every time we get into bed. That means as soon as we're done and we come out of the bedroom, you get in there and change the sheets, and take the others down to be washed. Got it?"

My dick pulsed in my pants. "Yes sir."

"You can thank Julian for that one, it was his idea. Nicer for us, plus he knew you'd appreciate it."

I nodded meekly, although inside I was ecstatic to have the confirmation that Julian still thought about my enjoyment, at least occasionally.

"As long as you're not busy on other jobs," Callum continued, "What I'd like is that when it sounds like we're close to being done, you should go get us water — iced, with some mint or lemon slices — and be ready outside the room so we can have a drink when we're done. And then when we get out of bed you can change the sheets."

I nodded vigorously, amazed that I was going to have the opportunity to stand outside the door when previously I'd just have to sneak the odd few minutes illicitly. "Yes sir," I said. "Thank you."

"You're welcome." He smirked a little; he obviously knew what this was doing to me. "Anyway, there's a bunch of food prep you'll need to do for dinner tonight. Johannes will be here about five thirty and he's left you a list of what he needs done before he arrives. But first you'll need to clean up in here."

I looked around the room. For a moment I didn't understand what he meant; I'd been meticulously careful unpacking, and there wasn't a thing out of place. But I understood as soon as Callum took his meaty cock in his hand, aimed it at my bed and started to release a stream of piss all over my blankets. As I stood there watching he waved his dick around, making sure he got piss everywhere. Then he shook it off, and walked out of the room without another word.

I guess I'd better get used to that, I told myself as I started pulling the wet sheets off the bed.

Once I was done changing the sheets and putting the urine-soaked ones in the wash, I headed to the kitchen to get the grocery list. That took me through the lounge, where I found Julian and Callum hanging out. Callum was sitting on a sofa checking his phone, while Julian was facing away from me, mixing drinks at the cocktail bar. He was naked except for a white jockstrap, his long blonde hair tied up behind his head. He was so muscular these days, I was constantly surprised. I was even more surprised to see his tattoo — a tramp stamp, just above the strap of his jock, in the shape of an X. Like on a pirate map. I wondered what it meant, till I remembered that Callum's last name was Cross. Julian had branded himself as Callum's property.

As I stood there, silent and unnoticed, Julian carried the drinks over. He handed one to Callum, then climbed onto Callum's lap, facing him. On his knees, he lowered his ass down onto Callum's crotch. They clinked their glasses together, and Julian started to grind his ass on Callum's crotch.

I cleared my throat nervously, guilty at disturbing their intimate moment. "I'm going to go get the dinner prepped," I announced. "Unless there's anything you need me to do for you before I get started?"

Without looking up at me Julian just said, "You only talk to us if we talk to you first. And you only come into the room if we call you."

"Sorry," I stammered. "I didn't realise."

"And don't stand there like a creep watching us."

"Of course. I'll leave you alone." I backed quickly out of the room. Neither of them acknowledged me, but as I left the room I heard Julian say quietly to Callum, "It's kinda hot putting him in his place like that. I see why you like it." They both laughed quietly.

I didn't see them much for the rest of the night. They had guests for dinner: a couple who were just as hot, handsome, stylish and perfect as Callum and Julian. I could hear them from the kitchen as I cleaned dishes; the group seemed relaxed with each other, and were having a great time. Julian slotted in so naturally, so comfortably into Callum's circle of friends that it was as though he'd always been there. I felt a pang of jealousy stab at me when I thought about how completely he'd moved on from me and found a home in Callum's life. But it also made me happy, knowing he was happy.

I came out a few times into the dining room to bring out food and clear the table, but not once did anyone acknowledge my presence or seem to notice I was there. I was literally nothing more than a servant to them.

After dinner they sat around drinking late into the evening. There was nothing left for me to do so I went upstairs and got ready for bed. As I brushed my teeth and washed my face, I planned out the following day: I'd get up, clean up the remnants of their party, bring them coffee, clean their sheets after they got out of bed. Their sweaty, musky, cum-stained sheets. I'd tidy, vacuum, mop, go to the florist to get fresh flowers for around the house. Prep lunch, prep dinner. Have my first session with the personal trainer so I'd eventually be able to look good for my new masters. And somewhere in there, if I was lucky, I'd get to stand outside their bedroom, listening to the sounds of their lovemaking while I waited with glasses of iced lemon-water for when they'd finished. Oh, and, change the sheets again. Thinking about it made my dick start to swell; even though it was a lot to do, and most of it was boring as hell, the idea of being their servant excited me. And the thought of getting to stand outside their door listening to them fuck made it all worthwhile.

As soon as I got into bed I fell asleep easily, exhausted by the adrenaline of my first day as a slave. But I woke up to the sound of car doors, and an engine as a car pulled away from the house. I smiled to myself; the guests were gone, and my husband and his lover would soon be coming up the stairs and heading to bed together. Which meant it wasn't long before they'd be wrapped in each other's arms, eyes locked on each other, and Callum would be entering Julian again, giving him yet another fuck that was beyond anything I could ever give him.

Sure enough, it wasn't long before I heard the sound of Julian moaning from the bedroom at the other end of the hall. I felt my dick harden, and I felt that familiar stab of jealousy in the pit of my stomach. But I smiled to myself, there in the darkness of my servant's quarters. The sound of Julian being fucked — really, thoroughly fucked — was the most beautiful sound in the world. The fact that he was being given that by someone else was my greatest fantasy come true. And the fact that I was here to hear it for myself, knowing that I was going to get to hear it every day for the rest of my life, was better than I could have ever imagined.